HOOD'S CAPER

FAIRYTALE BUREAU
BOOK ONE

EVE LANGLAIS

Hood's Caper © 2023 Eve Langlais

Cover by Addictive Covers © 2023

Produced in Canada

Published by Eve Langlais

http://www.EveLanglais.com

E-ISBN: 978 177 384 4954

Print ISBN: 978 177 384 4947

ALL RIGHTS RESERVED

This book is a work of fiction and the characters, events and dialogue found within the story are of the author's imagination and are not to be construed as real. Any resemblance to actual events or persons, either living or deceased, is completely coincidental.

No part of this book may be reproduced or shared in any form or by any means, electronic or mechanical, including but not limited to digital copying, AI training, file sharing, audio recording, email and printing without permission in writing from the author.

Prologue

The asteroid, too small for the NASA watchers to even bother with, mostly burned up as it came through the Earth's atmosphere. The heat turned the little rock a bright green, noticed only by Agatha Dunrobin as she sat on her back porch enjoying the evening air.

The old lady watched as the glowing speck in the sky plummeted, landing in her precious flowers. Alarmed for her prize-winning roses, Agatha clutched the handle of her cane with a gnarled, arthritic hand and thumped down the steps. As she hobbled toward her garden, she couldn't see the object at first, the foliage lush this time of year. She had to weave past thorny branches before she spotted a pulsing green glow. How odd. She'd always thought meteors glowed red like burning coals.

Agatha crouched, her joints protesting, but she ignored them to peer at the rock partially embedded in soil. A very round rock, smooth and glassy in appearance. The light from it emitted no heat when she waved her hand over it.

"How strange," she murmured aloud. It definitely didn't behave like a rock, even one from space.

Rather than grab it with her bare hand, she hobbled back to her basket of gardening supplies on the porch and snared her thick gloves before returning to pluck the object from the ground.

The stone, which felt heavier than expected and emitted no actual heat, continued to glow. Intrigued, she carried it inside for a better look. The bright glare of her kitchen lights didn't reveal any special details but rather emphasized its smooth, polished surface. It reminded her of jade, the green paler than an emerald but, unlike jade, more translucent. Putting on her bifocals, which she used for doing the daily crossword, she peered closer and spotted a tiny bright speck in the center.

How fascinating. Albert would have been over the moon if he'd found it.

Her late husband used to love hunting for geodes, and it brought a pang to think of how excited he would have been to discover this mystery in their garden. Thinking of him reminded her of his books. She'd not had the heart to get rid of them after his death, and they remained in the study, big dusty tomes about rocks that he used to read while they sat together in the evening.

The study—the place he used to grade papers from his students—had slowly become a hobby room, as knitting supplies now filled the desk he used to work at. The big club chair by the window, where Agatha sat and sometimes read, had a small side table holding her current book. A reproduction of *Children's and Household Tales*, written by the Brothers Grimm and first published in 1812. A dark tome of fairytales that hadn't been sanitized by modern times. It sat atop a modern version of adaptations. Agatha had been reading them both, studying their differences.

Agatha set the rock atop the book of fairytales while she perused the titles on the spines in the bookcase. Surely one of them would be able to name what she'd found.

A hum from behind lifted the hair on her nape, and she almost fell as she whirled quickly to see what caused it.

A blink of her eyes didn't change the fact that the rock she'd set down had flattened as if suddenly liquid, spreading across the cover of the book.

"Oh no!" she exclaimed. Without thinking, she reached to brush it away. An electrical shock stung her flesh. She snatched her hand away to hug it to her chest.

The green goo evaporated without staining the cover but left behind a tiny bright pebble, which sank into the book.

Then there was nothing. No glow. No rock. Not even a hole through the cover. Had she imagined it?

Agatha hesitated before grabbing the fairytale tome. A shiver went through her as she cracked it open to see if there'd been any damage. She found the grape-sized rock nestled in the heart of the book, sparkling faintly. As she watched, it literally sucked the words from the page, the texting sliding into the stone leaving the paper blank, which in turn increased the twinkling.

What kind of sorcery was this?

With a gasp, Agatha dropped the book back on the table, atop the brighter cover of the newer version. The jolt didn't stop the growth of light. It became big enough that the cover began to lift, revealing a fist-sized sphere of brilliance.

As fear replaced wonder, Agatha backed away, but it was already too late.

When the glowing ball exploded, the shockwave knocked her down. It took a moment to recover her wits and rise, only to realize something about her had changed.

She later discovered it wasn't just her. The entire world had been affected.

Fairytales began coming to life, cursing people to live out many of those terrible tales, made especially bad because these stories, written for a different time, clashed with the modern world. Eventually, it became known as the Grimm Effect and with it, a new era began, one of good and evil, magic and mayhem, happily ever afters, and tragedy.

1

The frog spat water, a big squirt that hit my leather jacket and dripped harmlessly but still annoyed.

I gritted my teeth. "Look here, you little green puke, you cannot stay in this fountain."

Croak. The frog disagreed.

"We've had too many complaints." Like, literally a dozen this morning alone about this amphibious jerk harassing all the women walking by, flicking his tongue at them, getting between their feet to peek up their skirts.

Ribbit.

"I don't care if you're cursed. You cannot try and tongue kiss everyone to try to reverse it. Besides, it won't work." Despite decades of living with the Grimm Effect, some folks still hadn't read the original stories, which were more horror than fairytale. "Come here, right this instant." I used my sternest voice and pointed to the fountain ledge.

Rather than obey, the frog chose to leap away from me—*sproing, sproing*—right in front of a car.

Apparently, he'd not played Frogger before his transformation because he didn't manage to avoid the sedan speeding past.

Splat.

The frog got flattened—literally squished into a puddle of green goo—which then expanded and expanded until a man lay naked on the pavement groaning, "Argh, I think I'm broken."

I headed for him and planted my hands on my hips as I huffed, "Next time, read a damned book. The frog wasn't cured by a kiss but by the princess getting peeved and tossing his ass against a wall."

"I need a doctor," he complained.

"And pants." Transformation spells were the worst when broken, as the person returned disoriented and naked. I put a call in to dispatch. "Frog problem resolved but the Grimpher"—the name given to a person caught up in the Grimm Effect—"requires medical assistance."

"On it," stated Darren, our guy manning the office phone line.

"What's going to happen to me?" whined the guy lying on the pavement.

"Nothing. Lucky for you, while annoying, you didn't harm anyone during the course of the curse, and now that it's broken, you can go back to your life. That is, once you get those bones set and do some rehab."

"But what about my princess? I was supposed to get a princess." He had the nerve to pout.

"Only the prince gets a princess in the book. And you, sir, are no prince."

With that, I left. Another mission accomplished. Although I would admit to being miffed that I didn't get to smack the frog myself. He'd tried to lick me on the lips with that nasty tongue of his when I'd first arrived. Almost lost it in the process. More annoying, this was the third frog I'd dealt with in the last month. I really hoped a true frog prince would find his damned princess and put that particular fairytale curse to bed, because that really was the only way to stop the cycle for a bit. See, since the Grimm Effect—also known as Fairytale Apocalypse and the Grimm Fuckeroo—through some kind of magic scientists couldn't explain, fairytales had been infecting people. One day, a girl walks to the store, dangling her basket, and the next thing, she's being stalked by a wolf and would have gotten eaten but for the handsome huntsman. Ask me how I know. It happened to my mother, and what do you know, the Little Red Cap curse was genetic. It passed down to me.

In high school, Dylan, a guy with wolfish intent, tried to corner me on my way home. A well-meaning kid named Nolan tried to step in and be my hero. Did I mention Nolan liked to hunt and wear plaid? Spotting the curse from a mile away, I kneed Dylan in the balls, broke his nose, and told him if he ever came near me again, I'd skin him for his fur. Then I told Nolan to take a hike. This Red Riding Hood didn't need a hero.

Breaking the fairytale mold, that was me, hence why the Fairytale Bureau hired me as part of their investigation and prevention unit. Those of us who bucked the trend made the best agents because we weren't afraid to stop a story dead in its tracks.

The bureau had a prime spot downtown, and I parked my motorcycle right in front on the sidewalk because a sign said no parking or stopping on the street. Would I get a ticket? Most likely not. Peter, the parking bylaw officer for this sector, had a crush on me. Contrary to what the boss said, I could play nice if necessary. I'd been known to smile for the guy at the sandwich shop so he'd load my sub with more meat.

I swung off my steel steed and removed my helmet, shaking out flame-red hair. All natural to my annoyance. Don't get me wrong. The color suited me, and I did love its vibrancy, but I hated how people acted when they saw it. Because they A) asked me if it came from a bottle, B) accused me of lying when I said it didn't, and C) snickered and said I must have a temper. I did and usually showed it at that point.

My briefcase, which the bureau insisted agents carry around, took only a second to unstrap from the rear fender. As to what it contained... A few items that could come in handy when in the field, such as a jar for capturing evil spirits—don't ask me how it worked. They just gave it to me with instructions to unscrew the lid in the presence of ghostly entities, of which I'd thankfully not yet met any. It also held a vial of holy water, which honestly didn't work on much, but it made some people feel better. There was a mirror for deflecting spells and evil stares. A silver dagger for stabbing things trying to kill me. Gold coins for bribing. Gems for the same reason—the irony being, in the post-Grimm-Effect world, those things lost all value except as bargains with monsters and tricksters. Oh, and my favorite to soothe savage beasts, the miniature harp I could play a single song on. "Twinkle, Twinkle, Little Star." At least I didn't have to sing, or I'd have been mauled for sure. My voice tended toward the huskier side. Blame the cigarettes I occasionally smoked, mostly to drive my mom wild.

With my briefcase case swinging from my hand, I strode inside the bureau, whistling. The boss wouldn't be too pissed with me this time. The frog would survive despite his injuries, I'd broken the spell, and, best of all, hadn't destroyed any public property.

Yet.

The day wasn't done.

As I walked in, Luanne glanced at me from behind the reception desk. "Hey, Hood."

They didn't call me that because I wore a stupid red cape—I didn't own a cloak, or anything red for that matter. However, I had the misfortune of being named Blanche Hood, courtesy of my granddad, Marcus Hood, an actual woodsman before the curse made it a thing.

"What's new and exciting?" I asked, pausing to chat.

Luanne was one of the few in our office who'd not defeated her curse. She'd been caught, but in a good, not bad way. She was currently married and popping out kids. A lot of kids, thanks to her fairytale, which was based on "The Twelve Brothers." For the moment, she'd birthed seven boys, and the plan was she'd get her tubes tied before she hit twelve, because the thirteenth child, if a girl, would result in the death of her sons. Did I mention the fact Grimm stories tended to be dark and very murderous?

Luanne leaned forward with an excited gleam in her eyes. "What's new? I'm surprised you didn't hear. We have a serial killer on the loose."

"Really? Since when?"

"Since this morning. Someone discovered a bunch of bodies in an old shack in the woods. Word is they were torn to pieces by a wild animal."

My brows raised. "Sounds like it might be a case for the bureau."

"Most likely," Luanne agreed. "I heard from Sally upstairs that Hilda was on the phone with the police chief."

"Then I guess I'd better get up there if I want to get assigned to the case." Unlike some, I didn't shirk jobs. I found satisfaction in solving cases and breaking curses. Not to mention, a serial killer sounded way more interesting than smashing another frog or cutting yet another wannabe-Rapunzel's hair. Funny how a simple snip was all it took to break that curse, which had the unfortunate side effect of turning the women into agoraphobics. The way they carried on after their trim, you'd think I cut off a limb. Apparently I'd ruined their chance at true love. Never mind the fact that, again, the world did not have enough princes for all these hopeful damsels. I never understood how some wanted the torture of being stuck inside, waiting to see if they'd be lucky enough to snare one of the rare royals caught in the same cursed storyline.

The Rapunzel one rarely ended well. Even decades later a fairytale that needed royalty wouldn't settle for a commoner. Although that might change. Rumor had it a few monarchies were offering to knight and give titles to those willing to pay big bucks. Would the curse recognize that they'd been anointed and not born? Guess we'd find out.

"If you find out any juicy details, do spill," Luanne said as I went on my way.

I ignored the elevator for the stairs. I didn't trust the box strung on the cable. It would be too easy for a fairytale curse to decide I needed rescuing. No thanks.

I took the steps two at a time and arrived on the third floor, only slightly huffing. Who needed a gym membership when I got all the exercise I needed for free? First floor held interview rooms, as well as a staging area for larger operations. Second floor was where we kept those who had to be detained, as well as our lockup for magical artifacts until they could be neutralized. Third floor held the main office, which bustled as agents—who happened to be Grimphers who'd beaten their curse—worked at various tasks.

You had Sally, who monitored for budding curses by watching social media for keywords. Tyrone, who kept track of former freed Grimphers to make sure they didn't fall right back into another story. Belle, Mahoney, and Judd were field agents like me, while Cinder in the corner handled any of the legal stuff that cropped up, like a homeowner trying to sue when I accidentally blew a hole in her roof getting rid of the goblins infesting her place.

At the far end of the chaos, the director's office. As I strode for it, Belle hissed, "I wouldn't go in there." Belle, like me, had also managed to foil the curse afflicting her. In her case, the beast proved unredeemable, and when she kept rejecting him, he tried to break into her house, which didn't end well for him. The case was a slam-dunk self-defense one, and she could now live without fear of getting stuck with a monster.

"I am totally going in because I hear there's a juicy crime scene that needs someone from our office."

"You might want to skip this one because, from the sounds of it, it might be a wolf," she divulged.

My brow arched. "Which is exactly my specialty." I'd spent my life studying them, even wrote my college thesis on wolves, so who better than me?

"I just don't know if you should be getting near any wolves."

I snorted. "I already told my wolf *and* the huntsman to take a hike." Despite Nolan being cute and well-meaning, I knew better than to sleep with him and give the curse anything to work with.

"You say that, and yet rumor has it the Grimm Effect is possibly evolving and is now trying to trick people who've managed to escape into a second shot."

I uttered a disparaging noise. "It can try all it wants. Not only will I send any wolf packing but anyone wearing plaid too." My dating profile on the app Not Looking for a Happily Ever After specifically stated no one in the forestry or wildlife industry. I wasn't about to end up suddenly bound in a magical curse that would fool me into thinking I was happy. I'd seen the results. Girls who'd been kissed awake out of a coma regretting the stranger they'd hooked up with, or the Snow Whites, pregnant and abandoned because they tended to be seduced by guys who liked the idea of a virgin in need of saving. So many didn't understand that, after the curse ran its course, the happily ever after part rarely lasted. On the contrary, I'd found most Grimm-induced relationships finished in violence, much like the original tales.

Was that to say everyone ended up miserable? No. I mean Luanne adored her husband. And my cousin beat the evil-stepmother curse and chose to love her stepkids rather than having them abandoned in the woods. But my mom... She'd let herself be seduced by the huntsman when he rescued her from the wolf, but he was a cad who left her pregnant and alone.

Now don't think I didn't believe in love, because I did. My grandmother loved my granddad, and he was pretty awesome until a tree fell on him in the woods. And before you ask, if a tree falls on you in a forest, you do scream, but even if heard, it doesn't help when your whole body is crushed.

Belle sighed. "I'm glad you're so confidant. I swear I've been on tenterhooks this past month waiting for a beast to appear."

I frowned. "You think your curse is active again?"

She shrugged. "I don't know. I just can't shake a feeling something's about to happen."

"You should try a distraction. You want first crack at this serial killer case?"

"No thanks." Belle grimaced.

Surprising since Belle had been bitching about the fact she kept getting the most boring cases. Like her most recent one where she helped a Grimpher spin gold so she wouldn't have to give away her baby to a guy named Rupert Stilt. His real name. I checked.

"You sure? Because if you need this case, it's yours."

"No way. I've got my vacation coming up."

"Ah yes, camping in the woods." I made a face. "Doesn't sound relaxing to me."

"I enjoy getting close to nature."

"Better you than me." And I meant it. My idea of relaxing had a pack of smokes, bottle of tequila, some good tunes, and a video game where I got to blow up zombies.

"Hood! My office. Now," Hilda bellowed, and I grinned.

"Looks like I am up. Sweet."

Despite what Belle cautioned, I was afraid of neither wolf nor curse. I'd beaten it once, and if it decided to come after me for round two, I'd shelve it again.

2

The briefing with Hilda didn't take long. She didn't yet have a file for me to read because the case was too fresh. What I received was an order to get my ass down to Regent Park and join the police as they catalogued the site where they'd found a bunch of bodies.

When I'd asked, "Any suspects?" Hilda's lips pinched. "Looks like an animal did it. Possibly a wolf. Is that a problem?"

"No, ma'am."

"Good because I need my best on the job. I'll expect a report before morning. You'll ignore your other pending cases until this one is handled."

Awesome news, seeing as how the cold cases I had would have kept me chained to my desk, calling up people and asking the same questions over and over. Boring!

Upon leaving the bureau, I hopped on my steel steed and scooted off, making good time. Regent Park proved easy to find with its armada of police cars and flashing lights. I wondered how many victims we were talking to elicit such a response. I showed my badge to the rookie manning the do-not-cross tape.

The rookie pointed. "The crime scene is in the midst of the woods, about a hundred yards that way."

I eyed the forest, thick and dense, an almost exact clone of the original Black Forest in Germany. Very old according to the people who studied it, which proved interesting, seeing as it had only been established a decade ago when the new suburb went in. But the Grimm Effect didn't care about things like natural growth. Whatever powered the curses created what it needed.

Some people had theorized that something must have been unearthed for this to have happened. That we'd unleashed some evil upon the world. I agreed. What no one knew was how to find it and make it stop. Hell, it took more than two decades of chaos before the bureau was even established to try to keep the stories and their ill effects in check.

I hiked into the forest, the outside noise quickly muffled as soon as I'd made it a few paces past the edge. The size of the trees proved impressive, the boles too wide to hug, covered in a gray-green moss. The branches were gnarled like some of the trunks.

Little light filtered through, just enough for me to

see. The path taken by the cops proved easy to follow, given the trampled foliage and a dropped evidence bag, but it was the smell of puke that let me know I neared the crime scene.

I emerged into a clearing that should have been sunny given the blue skies outside the forest, but somehow thick clouds hovered overhead. Police bustled around in the weed-infested yard that surrounded the falling-down hut. Some took pictures, and others plucked random items to seal in plastic bags. While the crime itself might be fairytale related, the bulk of the investigation—AKA analysis of evidence on-site—would be done by the cops on the off chance it turned out to be just a regular ol' psycho and not someone acting out a scene from a Grimm story.

A slender man in a suit stood talking to the police chief with a small fluffy dog tucked under his arm. It seemed rather incongruous given his size and appearance—tall, thick of shoulder, square-jawed, blond hair cut short. The suit glanced at me as I approached, and I was struck by his vivid blue eyes. Pretty boy. I wondered what he was doing out here in the woods.

Chief Patterson, whom I'd worked with before, noticed me and waved. "Hood, glad you could make it before we let our witness go."

I sauntered close, hands in my pockets, and drawled, "Came as fast as I could, Chief."

The police chief gestured. "This is Mr. Walden. He

was the one who called in to let us know about the bodies."

I eyed him up and down. "You don't look the type to be wandering around in a cursed forest." His leather loafers were more meant for pavement.

The handsome man shrugged. "I'd not planned to go hiking. Blame my furball. Rambo saw a bunny and slipped his collar to chase it into the woods. I followed and stumbled across this hut, which had my dog losing his mind. Usually, I would have just grabbed Rambo and left, but given he wouldn't stop growling and yipping, I thought I should see why and made the mistake of opening the door." He grimaced. "Kind of wished I hadn't."

"What did you see, Mr. Walden?" I asked, wanting to get his first impression while it remained fresh. The more time passed, the more witness details tended to change.

"The stench hit me before my eyes could figure out what I was looking at. I've never smelled anything so horrid." His lips twisted. "Then I saw the reason why."

Chief Patterson interrupted. "Tell her about the suspect."

"You saw who did it?" my sharp query.

"Maybe?" Walden shrugged. "Like I told the officers, I can't be sure what I saw. It happened so quick. While I stared in shock at the pile of bodies, motion caught my eye. By the time I glanced, I'd have sworn I saw the tail end of a wolf leaving through the back window."

"How do you know it was a wolf?"

"I don't," he admitted. "It could have been a large dog. Whatever it was, it had gray and black fur, a long tail, and a good-sized body."

"But you didn't see it actually killing anyone or chewing on parts?"

Walden shook his head. "No, and I'd rather not."

Understandable. "Do you live around here, Mr. Walden?"

He nodded. "Yes, I moved in a few months ago, about a mile from here. I've walked by this place dozens of times but never had an issue. And before you ask, I've never seen a wolf before. Just a few bunnies, which is how I ended up here."

The man sounded sincere and a little shaken. Understandable given what he'd stumbled across. "I assume you gave the officers your contact info in case we have more questions?"

"Yes. Although I'm not sure what else I can add."

"You might be surprised at the details you can remember later." Especially if questioned after making him drink some Candor Tea. Don't ever do that while drinking and playing Truth or Dare. I'd had a friend get dumped on the spot when the topic of best sex came up and she said her ex used to make her come multiple times at once. Me, I admitted that I never wanted to fall in love. The truth to this day.

"In that case, here's my card... Ms. Hood?" He said it questioningly.

"Actually, it's Agent Hood with the Fairytale Bureau, investigative department."

"Nice to meet you, Agent Hood. Now if I'm done here, could I go home? I'd like to toss back a few whiskeys and try to forget what I saw and smelled today."

"You're free to go, Mr. Walden." Patterson waved him off.

I watched him walk away before tuning in to what Patterson was saying. "...your impression."

I clued in real quick. "You want me to go in there?" My nose wrinkled. It should be known I wasn't squeamish. I was the girl who would take a live worm and stab it on a fishing hook. Who could hunt a turkey in the fall, pluck it, gut it, and brine it for cooking. But exploring a massacre that stank? Not high on my list. Regardless, a picture would never do this travesty justice, not to mention images didn't give me a chance to walk the crime scene and truly get a feel for what might have happened.

"Got a mask?" My kit lacked the necessary equipment, since I didn't normally investigate scenes with decaying bodies, but I knew better than to walk into a place making experienced cops puke without something to block the smell. Not to mention, I didn't want to taste it when I breathed.

Patterson snapped his fingers, and one of his plebes scurried over with a shoulder bag.

"Equip Agent Hood so she can go inside." Equipping meant more than a face covering to help with the stench. There was also the menthol compound that made my eyes water when applied under my nostrils. Then there was everything that would ensure I didn't contaminate the scene: booties to go over my combat boots and gloves for my hands. As if I planned to touch anything.

I slid past the partially ajar door and stood just within for a second. Mr. Walden must have had a strong stomach to have been able to withstand the odorous carnage. The potent menthol rub didn't quite mask it. Odd how I'd not smelled it outside, given the cracks in the siding. I made a note to have Sally return and check for spells.

Next, the massacre itself. I couldn't have said how many bodies were piled inside. They'd been stacked every which way. Not all in one piece either.

A body at the front lacked an arm and one leg below the knee. A stray arm lay a few feet from the pile but didn't appear to match. The wounds on the bodies appeared ragged and savage. As if torn apart by a wild animal.

Or a wolf.

I edged closer and crouched down before stating, more as an observation than anything, "Is it me, or is there no biting or chew marks?"

The guy in a full bodysuit taking pictures paused to say, "Didn't need to chomp them to kill."

"But why kill them if not to eat them?" I pointed out.

"Because whatever did this is a killer."

The easy answer but I knew better. I'd studied wolves. Yes, they did kill to protect the pack and defend themselves. But most times when they hunted it was to feed, not just for the sake of killing. However, if this were part of a Grimm story, then it could be plausible. The wolf in "The Seven Young Kids" did eat the children without provocation. In "Little Red Cap," which some called "Red Riding Hood," he was bad as well. The wolves in all the stories were, and I'd know. I'd made it part of my college thesis to document them all.

Some might say that perhaps a regular rabid wolf had done this. I'd disagree. A normal wolf would have killed them and left them at the site of the kill, not dragged them to hide in a hut.

I did a circuit of the small shack, which was long abandoned if I went by the dust and grime. I spotted a broken chair and lopsided table. The bed was just a frame. There were no personal items. No clothing, pictures, or even knickknacks. Just a spooky hut in a spooky forest that most likely just appeared one day.

A window caught my attention, as it was the only one that had its shutters open. It had to be the one Mr. Walden claimed to have seen the wolf—or large dog—escaping from. Interesting how not a single strand of hair got caught on the sill. No claw marks either. Not impossible, of course. A large-sized canine could have simply leaped and not had to pull itself over the ledge. An open window explained how it got in and out, but if it were the killer, how had it gotten the bodies in here if the door was closed?

Another oddity struck me. I flipped around to eye the room with a frown.

"What's wrong?" asked the photographer.

"Where's the flies?" Decomposing meat should have been covered with the swarming fuckers.

The guy shrugged. "This whole forest doesn't have a normal ecosystem, so is it really that surprising?"

It led to me making another mental note to have Sally do a spell-check, not just on the lack-of-smell situation—because an open window should have aired out the reek for at least a few yards around—and the lack of usual decay. Maggots, flies, even local wildlife should have been having a heyday with this rotted feast.

With nothing to see, since I couldn't exactly touch the bodies, I exited to see Patterson talking to someone, who then moved off at a brisk pace.

"So?" he asked.

"Definitely a murder scene," my deadpan reply.

"Any ideas on who or what we're looking for?"

"Mr. Walden seemed to think a wolf or a dog."

"Bah. We both know a dog wouldn't have piled them up nice and tidy. Wolf either."

"A werewolf might have." The Grimm Effect had

changed one aspect of the story in that the wolf in "Little Red Cap" was literally a man who became a wolf. AKA a werewolf.

"Werewolves are usually smarter," he opined.

True. They didn't want to get shot. "I'd say anything willing to massacre people on that scale lacks a few brain cells." I paused before saying, "Do you have any suspects?"

"Not yet. Too soon. Once we sift some of the evidence, maybe we'll find some traces of DNA."

Which would help, as everyone these days had to donate to the registry. It became necessary when the curse sometimes changed people physically to the point they couldn't be recognized. Upon birth, nurses now took blood for the regular tests and the DNA bank.

"I'll see if the office has any wolves or other known folks with great big claws on file in the area," I mentioned.

"You think it's someone local?" Patterson asked.

"Someone not from around here wouldn't have known about this hut and most likely would have left the bodies scattered. This seems more like the killer felt this was a safe spot for them. I doubt too many people go for casual strolls in these woods."

Patterson shook his head. "Even my own guys didn't want to come in here. Said it was haunted."

"I assume you'll have some of your task force going door to door asking if people saw anything?"

"Already got the rookies on it. I'll have the report sent to your office. If you find something, be sure to send it over," Patterson stated.

"Sure thing, Chief," I said, lying through my teeth. We only passed on pertinent info for non-Grimm crimes. Other than that, we tended to handle the cases ourselves. Not everyone had the guts to smash a frog, behead a monster, or hold down a girl to cut her hair. I did.

Because the alternative was letting the curse win, and I didn't like to lose.

3

WITH NOT MUCH ELSE TO DO IN THE WOODS, I headed home for a shower. I needed to sluice the smell of death from my skin, hair, and clothes.

I lived in a three-story apartment complex, to my mom's chagrin. She harped weekly about me moving out. She and my grams lived in a cute cottage on the outskirts of town. It ran on a well and septic, which caused countless issues and were costly to repair. The electricity pole kept getting knocked down because they'd put it in a bad spot. The roof occasionally leaked no matter how many guys we had out to check it. But would Mom move? Nope. She kept hoping my sperm donor—AKA the supposed love of her life—would find her. Thirty-five years later and I was pretty sure she needed to move on.

But the constant maintenance wasn't the real reason I wouldn't move in. I needed my own space, and while cramped, I loved the privacy of my one-bedroom, somewhat compact apartment. No one to get annoyed when I gamed until three a.m. No one to complain when I piled my dirty clothes on the floor.

I entered and sighed in relief as the chaos of the world receded in the face of my monochrome décor. My hair might be flaming red, but everything else I owned? Mostly black, with some white or gray. Call it me rebelling against nature.

I had no pets, at all, unlike Cinder, who lived with a bunch of mice. On purpose, I should add, not because she had a rodent problem. She tended to attract small animals. The mice kept her place bug-free. Birds often brought her berries. A local raccoon liked to steal flowers for her.

Me, I had a large-screen television, a gaming system, a fridge full of microwave dinners, and a vibrator to keep me company. Life couldn't get any better.

I shed my clothes and hit the shower, sluicing off the grime of the day. I soaped, I shampooed, and only as I rinsed suds from my eyes did I notice my tub filling with water, the drain once more misbehaving. The problem with an older place. The plumbing often sucked.

My plunger took some vigorous pushing and pulling before the clog cleared with a satisfying whoosh. With my body wrapped in a towel, I was headed for my bedroom when someone pounded at my door.

I ignored it. People had to be buzzed into the building, and since I'd not let anyone in, I wasn't about to answer. I threw on a sweatshirt and some track pants as the incessant knocking continued.

Persistent bugger. "For Grimm's sake," I huffed. I stomped to the door and peered through the peephole to see a massive chest. Like really wide.

Bang. Bang. Bang.

The whole door shook. I pursed my lips and snapped, "Go away. Whatever you're selling, not interested."

"Not selling shit. Your apartment is leaking into mine," grumbled a deep voice.

"Sounds like a building maintenance problem," I opined.

"I *am* fucking maintenance. Something is leaking from your place through my bathroom ceiling."

His statement reminded me of my earlier plunging. Uh-oh. Had something busted when I did it?

"How do I know you're really the repair guy for the building?"

"Jesus fucking Christ. Call Larry and ask him. Tell him Aidan is at your door, and while you're at it, you could mention you're being difficult."

"It's not being difficult. It's called being safe. For all I know, you're a psycho."

"Would a psycho knock in plain view of everyone else on the fucking floor?"

"Sounds like something a psycho would say to convince me they aren't crazy." Yeah, I screwed with him. When it came to bullies, I never gave an inch and swung back just as hard.

"A free apartment in exchange for my services is really not worth dealing with this shit," he grumbled.

For some reason, that comment cinched it for me. I flung open the door and crossed my arms to say sweetly, "Ah, sugar, maybe it's your sweet demeanor that gets you those kinds of reactions."

He glared at me. "I don't do sweet."

"Or polite either," I remarked.

"You going to let me in to check, or should I just call Larry and tell him to evict your ass because your apartment is no longer considered safe for habitation since I had to shut off the water and initiate mold remediation?"

My mouth rounded. "You wouldn't dare."

"Your apartment is leaking into mine. Fucking right I will. Also, mold is no joke, and neither is drywall repair. Takes forever to clean up the dust."

"Well, since you're asking so nicely..." I swept a hand. "The bathroom is that way."

"I know where it fucking is. Every apartment is laid out the same." He stomped his way past me in his molding T-shirt tucked into snug but worn jeans.

"Hey! Shoes!" I yelled as he tromped over my clean floors.

"They're indoor shoes, Red. So calm your ass down. They ain't dirty."

"Says you," I muttered under my breath.

"Yeah, says me," he replied, somehow hearing me.

I frowned and followed to find him fiddling with the shower knobs. "Where's your tools, Mr. Fix it?"

"In the maintenance closet. Ain't no point lugging them all up here until I know what I need." He ran a finger along the caulking. Patted his hands along my floor.

I cleared my throat. "Um, I had to plunge the drain again. Could the leak have come from there?"

He cast me a glance. "Hairball issue?"

I gaped at him. "I am not shedding that bad."

"Doesn't matter. A few strands here and there accumulates." He leaned into the tub, and his jeans pulled even tauter. Nice ass. Pity he was a jerk.

He grunted. "Un-fucking real."

"What?"

"You somehow managed to plunge hard enough to disconnect the drainpipe." He couldn't hide his incredulity.

"What can I say? I don't know my own strength."

He rose and towered. "This is going to be a pain in the ass to fix."

"But you can fix it, right?"

He nodded. "Yeah. But it won't happen today. I'm

going to need to buy some shit for the repair. I'll cut a hole in my ceiling to access the problem and pray I can fix it that way, or we're gonna have to rip out the tub."

I blinked. "Because of a loose pipe?"

"You disconnected it, Red. As in, right now, any water going down that drain is just pouring into my place. Which means no more showers until it's fixed."

"Excuse me? I kind of need to shower."

"Then do so at a neighbor or friend's place."

"That's not exactly convenient. Shouldn't the management of the building be comping me a hotel until it's fixed?"

"Not when it's your fault it's broken," he countered.

My lips pursed. "I didn't do it on purpose. I just wanted to clear a clog."

"You should have snaked the clog. Or called me."

"Well, I know that now," I grumbled.

"Are you going to be around tomorrow?"

"Why?"

"Because I'll be coming in and out of your place to fix it, that's why."

"I'm going to be at work."

"In that case, do I have permission to enter during your absence so I can get started?"

"Do I have a choice?" I groused.

"Depends on if you want to ever bathe again or not."

"Fine," I huffed. "But no coming in between 8 p.m. and 8 a.m."

"Is that when your boyfriend comes over?"

"No." I snorted. "It's when I relax from my day and sleep, you moron. Once I head to the bureau, I'm usually gone until late afternoon."

"Which bureau you work for? With your attitude, I'm going to guess the DMV."

"Ha, so funny," I scoffed. "Actually, I'm with the Fairytale Bureau."

He recoiled. "You're one of them?"

"An agent, yes," my dry reply. Some people had this weird thing about us, as if even just conversing would cause them to be cursed next. Not the way it worked. Actually, no one knew how the Grimm Effect chose people.

"I'll work on it tomorrow when you're gone," he muttered, heading for the door.

"Will it be fixed by dinner?"

"Depends on how well it goes, so no showers until I tell you it's good," he admonished before leaving.

Pleasant fellow. Obviously new since I'd met the last maintenance guy. Maurice of the giant belly, who came to replace my leaky faucet last year and had to have me help him since he couldn't fit under the sink.

With the oh-so-pleasant Aidan gone, I turned on the news and grabbed my phone. As the subject of the murders in the woods came up, I paused my scrolling of social media to listen.

The announcer knew less than me. She kept the report to unidentified bodies found in the woods, no suspect yet, but she did mention the possibility of wolf involvement.

Could it be a wolf? I wondered. Some of the facts didn't add up. The closed door for instance. Unless the wolf shifted to his man shape to open it and then shifted back to wolf before he left.

And who were the victims? I'd seen men and women in the pile, so the killing wasn't sex-based. I couldn't have said the average age, though. Too much blood and decomposition for that.

What of the guy who'd found it, Mr. Walden? Shaken but composed all at once. I still didn't get the dog. He seemed like the type to own a large breed, not a tiny fluffy lap thing. Could be his wife's or girlfriend's. His story sounded plausible, though. A dog might have smelled what we couldn't, hence how Walden was led there.

My phone rang, and without glancing, I knew who called. Only one person had the circus-theme ringtone.

"Hi, Mom."

"Baby girl!" My mom always sounded so cheery to hear my voice. "It's been ages."

"We talked two days ago."

"So much can happen in two days," she gushed.

"Oh really? What happened?"

"Nothing, but something could have," she insisted.

"Is there a point to this call? It was a long day."

Not entirely true, but my frozen dinner awaited, as did a few hours of virtual zombie slaying.

"I'm making your favorite for dinner..." she sang.

Okay, that perked me up. "Steak sandwiches?"

"Yup, it's all prepped and ready to cook if someone is interested."

"On my way." Fuck zombies. I'd kill them later. No one ever said no to Mom's steak sandwiches. Tender slices of beef, not too thick, flash-fried in some mixture that had garlic, salt, pepper, and some weird sauces I couldn't have named. She layered it on a garlic butter toasted bun, along with fried mushrooms, onions, green peppers, melted mozzarella, and then the weird but tastiest part, chopped lettuce with Italian dressing. Tangy, salty, crunchy, and tender all at once. I drooled as I headed out of my place for the twenty-minute drive to my mom's.

As I gunned my machine, the sky remained bright, the late summer sun not setting for another hour still. I'd have to ride back in the dark, or I could spend the night. My mom kept my room untouched in case I wanted to move back in. Not happening, but I did appreciate the thought.

While the forest with the murder scene resided on the other side of the city, I couldn't help but eye askance the copse of trees I passed as I hit the burbs. None of them old and gloomy like Regent Park, but that could change if the Grimm Effect decided it had a use for them.

The whole magic thing used to be a concept unknown, at least according to my mom, Grams, and history books. The world used to not worry about suddenly being dragged into a storyline that wanted them to be a certain thing. Didn't have issues with witches and monsters. Didn't worry about magic changing the very fabric of reality. Some wished fervently the Grimm Effect would disappear. I wasn't one of them. This had always been a part of my life. Me against the curse that tried to force me into its version of a happily-ever-after. Or the Grimm version of The End.

Lives had been ruined by it, but some enriched as well. I know Luanne claimed to be super happy, although I had to wonder if that would last when she got her tubes tied and the curse couldn't make her have any more babies.

My mom certainly didn't emerge a winner. She'd indulged in a grand love affair, which turned out to be fleeting. Sure, she claimed that having me was all that really mattered, but I saw the sadness in her eyes during her lonely moments. I wish she'd meet another dude—I'd even have settled for a new huntsman—to sweep her off her feet. Alas, Mom pined for the man who ditched her and never once looked back.

The lane I turned down had glowing moonlight to guide me to the cottage, which looked adorable, as always. A stone exterior with white accents, like the wood trim around the windows and doors. The cedar-shingle roof of an orangey-brown hue went well with the garden backdrop. Mom did have a way with plants, which Grams claimed skipped her in favor of her daughter and older sister. I'd never met my great-aunt with the green thumb, as she lived overseas. Since the Fairytale Apocalypse, flying became too risky and expensive on account of the planes needing accompanying fighter jets to deter dragons.

Yes, dragons.

Apparently they used to be considered myth. No longer, and they could be very territorial about the skies.

I parked my bike and had barely taken off my helmet when the door opened and Mom screeched, "Baby girl!"

"Jeezus, Mom. I saw you on the weekend." She'd made fresh spaghetti sauce and sent me home with several premade containers for meals. I didn't care how strange I looked with a cooler strapped to my bike.

"Can't a mother be delighted to see her most perfect daughter?" Mom clasped her hands and beamed.

Grams cleared her throat. "A perfect granddaughter wouldn't be riding that death trap." Grams, bless her heart, did not approve of my motorcycle. Or my clothes. Or my lack of a husband and kids. But apart from that, she was rather awesome—and taught me everything I knew about fleecing at poker.

"You only say that because you haven't ridden in so

long. Hop on and I'll take you for a ride and prove to you that age is just a number. Next thing we know, you'll be wearing chaps as you go travelling cross country, picking up burly dudes with giant beards called Moe."

Without missing a beat, Grams replied, "I do have a bustier that does great things for my tits."

A normal mom would have been traumatized to hear my seventy-five-year-old Grams talking about her boobs. Mine encouraged it. "It does. And those jeans you have do great things for your ass. Speaking of ass, have you lost weight, baby girl?"

I almost rolled my eyes. "No, Mom, I have not lost a single pound."

"You look pale. Are you getting enough sunshine?" The interrogation continued as we went inside, the interior as eclectic and cozy as the exterior. The furniture didn't match at all, the couch and chair completely different styles and fabric, which clashed with the patterned wallpaper and striped rug. The dining room had a good-sized wooden table with six chairs, all different. The kitchen cupboards at least had been painted to match, but then Mom had decorated them using stencils, the bright splash of colors almost more than my monochrome-loving heart could take. A shrink would take one look at the home I'd grown up in and my apartment now and probably say, "It makes sense."

The idle chitchat lasted while Mom fried up

dinner. I didn't say a word as I devoured two of the sandwiches, which she served with freshly made kettle chips sprinkled with salt and vinegar.

The amount of food ingested required me to pop the button on my jeans in order to fit in the dessert of upside-down pineapple cake. Also a favorite. Mom did spoil me in the best way.

I sighed as I relaxed afterwards in the living room, almost drowsing in food-coma satiation. That was until Mom blurted out, "I hope you're not going anywhere near those murders."

My eyes popped open. "Why?"

"I've got a bad feeling about it." Mom chewed her lower lip.

"It'll be fine."

"Are you saying you are?" Mom squeaked.

"Kind of don't have a choice since I'm the investigating agent."

"Can't you turn it over to someone else?" Mom pled.

"You heard the girl. It's her job. Was it as gruesome as they said on the news?" Grams had bright inquiring eyes.

"Very gross."

"Who could do such a thing?" Mom paced and wrung her hands. "How awful. Those poor families."

"At least they'll get closure," I stated. So many families didn't. The amount of people missing every year could be staggering. As the curse took them on wild quests, many of them fatal, some folks never knew what happened to loved ones.

"They were saying it might be a wolf," Grams stated.

"That's not been confirmed."

"A wolf?" Mom perked up. "I don't suppose there's a huntsman involved too?"

"No, there is not," I replied firmly. "So you can stop thinking this is the Grimm Effect trying to ensnare me again."

Mom's lips turned down. "Who says I wanted the huntsman for you?"

"Oh, Mom..." It did hurt me to dash her hope.

She clapped her hands, once more smiling brightly. "Cards anyone?"

"I really should get back. I've got an early start in the morning." Not entirely true. None of the agents had set times to be in the office. We were expected to do our jobs, and since those sometimes could have us keep weird hours, we went in when we wanted. For me, that was usually after nine so I could sleep in. But knowing I'd have the police report to check over, I planned on being there earlier.

I hugged my family goodbye and set off on my bike, the night sky barely visible over the city lights as I neared my neighborhood. I parked in my spot and headed for the entrance. A glance upwards showed my windows dark but the one below it illuminated, and a figure standing silhouetted. A big figure.

My ornery neighbor. It bugged me to know he'd be coming in my place while I wasn't there. Not that I feared theft, more that he might snoop in my things. I'd once lived in a place where the landlord used to go through my underwear drawer. I'd tossed them all once I found out and moved. I also anonymously reported the perv to the cops, and what do you know—his apartment and hard drive held enough to have him charged.

As I neared the locked entrance to my building, a shadow moved, and I halted, my hand dropping to reach into my jacket. While I only brought my briefcase on official business, I never went out, even casually, without a gun.

A low teasing note preceded the man stepping into the light, a fiddle held in the crook of his shoulder and neck. He played a sad song and stared at me intently. From the streetlight, I could see his fingers bandaged, his expression mournful. Cursed and somehow led to me.

"What do you want?" I asked, not relaxing my guard.

"I hate music," he whispered. "But I cannot stop playing." Of course he couldn't. He'd been caught in "The Strange Musician" tale. The man would fiddle endlessly, drawing wild animals to him, which would then also try to kill him. It wasn't a story with an ending. The musician kept travelling, playing, until he died. A cruel curse with only one solution.

I strode for him and ripped the violin from his grip and smashed it upon the ground. Over and over until it was just mangled wood and strings.

The man stared at me.

"You're welcome," I stated.

"But—"

"Stay away from music shops and places with instruments and you'll be fine."

His mouth opened and closed before he whispered, "Thank you," and ran off.

If only they could all be so simple.

4

THE NEXT MORNING, MY ALARM WOKE ME AT the ungodly hour of seven. Ugh. I would have liked to sluice off, given I'd tossed and turned and gotten a bit sweaty, but my tub remained out of order. I did my best with a sink bath, using a facecloth to wipe down and then misting with something called Vanilla Bean Haze. Blame my mom for me even owning body spray.

I headed to the bureau and greeted Luanne on the way in, who waved as she spoke on the phone. I then said hello to Cinder and Belle, who'd arrived before me.

They clustered around my desk to pepper me with questions.

"I heard the hut in the woods was a slaughterhouse," Belle stated. "Glad I didn't go. I'd have hated to puke on my new shoes."

"That's what the paper bootie protectors are for," I replied.

"I'm good."

"Looks like the morgue conducting the autopsy is having a hard time with the slashes." Cinder must have peeked at my report. I didn't mind. She was better with the paper-trail forensic stuff than me. "They look like an animal clawed them, but the depth of the cuts and their randomness are also contradicting it—let alone the absence of bite marks."

"Could be something we've never seen before," Belle opined as I booted up my computer.

"A new story?" Cinder didn't hide her skepticism. "I thought it was pretty established that only the original tales from the 1812 book and some adaptations were the ones being reenacted."

"And who's to say that can't change?" Belle interjected. "No one knows how the Grimm Effect came about in the first place. Why can't it evolve or expand to other books?"

"Don't even think it," Cinder huffed. "Can you imagine if it decided to use one of the bibles? A flood would kill just about everyone."

"I'd be more worried about it latching onto Stephen King's or Clive Barker's stuff," I murmured.

The very suggestion widened their eyes. "That would be horrifying," Cinder breathed.

"Literally," I replied, deadpan, before opening my email to look for the report. "I assume, given your comments on the cuts, that we have something from the police department?"

"Not much. The autopsies will continue today, as will the analysis of fluids and other detritus. No suspects. No motive. No link between the victims," Cinder summarized.

She would be correct. Basically, the report detailed what I'd seen. Pile of dead bodies in a shack in the woods. No physical evidence to tie anybody. Not yet. They were still running lab tests on specimens, IE fingernail scrapings, dust, and dirt from the floor sweepings. I did scroll back a page as something I skimmed over caught my eye.

"What's got you looking so serious?" Belle leaned closer to read my screen.

"The clothing the victims wore." I pointed. "Is it me, or is there a lot of red fabric in there?" At the time, I'd not paid attention to the victims' garments, nor noticed the amount of red given all the dried and dark blood caking them.

"Seven shirts in total, six of them red. And a red skirt," Belle muttered.

Whereas Cinder murmured, "Uh-oh."

I knew what she thought, and immediately issued my disagreement. "This isn't at all related to the Little Red Cap story."

"But it looks like it might be a wolf, and they all wore red," Cinder insisted.

"And? There are other stories with wolves."

"Wolves that eat people?" Belle countered. "You remember what I told you yesterday about curses reactivating for some people who evaded? I wouldn't discount it so quickly."

"Well, if it is the wolf, and he comes after me, he won't live to regret it." I wouldn't hesitate to shoot.

"I guess the bigger question is, did you meet a handsome huntsman?" Cinder grinned as I grimaced.

"No. And even if I did, I would run the other way. I will not become a victim."

"Not everyone hates their fairytale ending," Cinder countered.

"Says the woman who wouldn't put on the shoe when the prince came around."

Her lips twisted. "Prince Henrick was almost seventy. Why do you think I lost it in the first place? I was escaping his groping hands." Cinder had gone to a charity masquerade ball in her early twenties. While she didn't have a wicked stepmother or sisters to contend with, she did have jealous coworkers, who found out she was planning to go because of a free ticket she'd won on a radio contest. Having picked up her dress from the seamstress on her way to work, she'd hung it in the lunchroom, where the jealous cows did a number on it. When they left, Cinder wept over it as a last customer entered. You might have guessed who—a fairy godmother, who made it so Cinder could still go.

And she'd looked amazing. I'd seen the pictures. Dancing the night away. Drawing the eye of the ancient prince in attendance.

But she'd avoided what came after, never trying on

the shoe when he came looking for her. One of her coworkers put it on instead and married the prince. She later died when the prince found out she'd lied, something about treason to his throne. A smart Cinder—not her real name but the one given to her by coworkers which she happily adopted as a badge of honor—had escaped the curse.

"I don't need a man, huntsman or otherwise, to make me happy," I vehemently stated.

"I wish I had that dilemma," Belle groused. "I'd prefer something that isn't battery-powered."

I snorted. "Or hairy."

She grimaced. Her initial beast had been furry head to toe. "Don't even remind me. You know, in the stories, they made it seem like love cured him, but they never mentioned that love involved sex with a virgin." Even worse, not all the women survived that coupling. Sometimes the beast got a little too enthusiastic.

"Back to the case... I don't think it has anything to do with me or a different Red Cap in the area."

"Why not?" Belle glanced at me with a curious yet doubtful look.

"Because in the story of Little Red Cap the wolf didn't collect bodies," I explained. "It ate the grandma, and wanted to eat the girl. In this case, our perpetrator isn't ingesting victims."

"So which story do we think it is? Quite a few of them have psycho killers," Cinder mused aloud.

"I don't recall any of them storing corpses, though," Belle countered.

My memory was hazy on that score too.

Cinder glanced at me. "What's your next move?"

I shook my head. "I don't know."

"What about that witness? The one who found it?" Cinder leaned over to drag my cursor to a different page and then highlighted his address. "Says he thought he saw a wolf or a dog leaving the hut."

"I already spoke to him."

"While he was in shock. You should visit him again now that he's had a chance to process. I know when I'm building a case, oftentimes, what the initial report details and what they later remember can differ." Cinder made a good point.

Still... "Meaning he'll have had time to convince himself it was, indeed, a wolf."

"If it was, there will be something to confirm once the rest of the lab tests come in. A wolf sheds dander and hair, and it leaves behind saliva in the wounds." Cinder ticked off the many ways it could have left a clue.

"I guess since I have no other leads..."

Guess I'd be paying Walden a visit.

His house did prove to be close to Regent Park. A nice place, not quite mansion-sized but at least three or four bedrooms. Red brick exterior with black shutters, window trim, and a glossy door. The two-car garage had no windows, so I couldn't see if he'd parked inside it. The spotless driveway held nothing, not even a grease spot.

The front lawn appeared tidy, as did the garden beds. I couldn't imagine Mr. Walden tending either. He most likely hired out.

A knock at the door didn't bring anyone to answer. No Mrs. Walden. No housekeeper. Also, no dog barking.

I frowned at the frosted glass. I thought little mongrels yapped at everything. Maybe he'd trained it to not do that, or he'd taken it to work.

A few steps back and I craned, looking upward, though not sure what I sought. Whatever it was, I didn't find it. The house looked normal. The neighborhood as well. No rapidly spreading rose bushes, indicating a Beauty tale. No gnarly encroaching forest of candied house stories.

With my status as agent for the bureau, I didn't need a warrant to peek in his backyard. I just couldn't enter his house without just cause.

The yard proved plain. Perfectly mowed lawn. A stone patio, lacking furniture, that had a sliding glass door leading into the house. I walked the length of the yard, and it took me a second to realize that not only did the lawn lack little poop bombs but I also didn't see any yellow spots where the dog pee had killed the grass. Mom was always cursing about the neighbor's pooch who kept pissing in the same spot. Could be Mr. Walden walked his dog to preserve his yard.

Since the home visit proved a bust, I checked my phone to see he didn't work too far, the address not one I'd visited before. Might as well go and say hello.

With my motorcycle clamped between the thighs, giving me a nice thrill, I made my way to a busy location where the sun had a hard time getting past all the tall office buildings. The one I sought proved to be one of the largest. At least thirty stories of reflective glass, which explained the bird that smacked into it and fell. Not the first that morning by the looks of the corpses on the ground below.

I headed inside, passing through the glass doors, only to be stopped by security at the screening station when I failed to produce a building pass.

The corpulent fellow hiked his pants and kept his thumbs tucked in the loops as he confronted me. "Hello, ma'am. Who do you have an appointment with?"

"I don't."

"Then I'm afraid I'll have to ask you to leave."

While I usually didn't flex, I also didn't like people obstructing me when I worked. I yanked out my badge and flashed it. "Agent Hood with the Fairytale Bureau, here to speak to Mr. Walden about a current investigation."

"Is he in trouble?" the guard asked, looking a tad eager.

"No, just doing a follow-up."

"Oh." Now he seemed disappointed. "Is he expecting you?"

"Nope." I popped the p. "I thought I'd surprise him. But before I do, what can you tell me about Mr. Walden?"

"I'm not supposed to talk about the buildings' occupants." A stiff, well-practiced reply.

"Obviously you can't with normal people. But we're both in the security and law enforcement field." I fed his ego. "One pro to another, what can you tell me?"

He leaned in close to whisper, "He's a stiff one. Never says hello. He comes in every day, same time, eight a.m. Leaves at five o'clock exactly."

"What's the name of his company?" I probably could have looked it up, but asking would be quicker.

"Walden Inc."

Well, that didn't tell me much. "And what does his company do?"

The security guard shrugged. "No idea. He's only been here a few months. You're the first person who's shown up to see him."

My brows arched. "That seems odd."

"Not really. Since the plague of 2020, lots of folks are doing things virtually." A plague caused by rats that were, you guessed it, cursed.

"If he has no clients, then why the expensive office?"

He shrugged. "No idea. Maybe to escape the wife

at home?" He then seemed to realize how that sounded and blustered, "Just saying some people like a quiet office atmosphere and no distractions."

I didn't bust his balls over it since he fed me information. "What about Mr. Walden's dog?"

His confusion matched his, "What dog?"

So he didn't bring it to work. "I should go speak with him. What floor is he on?"

"Top one. He rented the entire thing."

Extravagant for a guy who didn't have any clients that visited. "Thanks." I headed for the elevator despite my general dislike of them. Even my fit butt wasn't about to climb thirty flights of stairs.

The elevator music had me tapping my foot in boredom and impatience. When the doors slid open, I stepped out to see nothing.

Not entirely true. The vast open space had a few columns going to the ceiling. Windows all around let in sunlight, bright enough I squinted. What I didn't spot? Any desks. Or boxes. Or anything you'd expect to find in an office, just concrete floors and drywall needing paint.

"Can I help you?"

The familiar voice had me turning to see Walden coming around the side of the elevator, which projected through the middle of the building.

"Hello, Mr. Walden."

"Agent Hood. What a pleasure to see you again." I didn't sense any fakeness in his greeting or nervousness. On the contrary, his wide grin almost made me smile in reply.

I didn't cave to his charm. "I wanted to talk to you again about yesterday's incident. Is it a good time?"

"Even if it weren't, I'd make time for you." He definitely flirted.

Don't get me wrong. Totally flattered, but still, I'd come on official business. "Were you working?"

"Not exactly. I was just studying the blueprints for the remodel. Wanted to make sure everything I asked for was included before handing it over to the construction crew."

"What are you turning this area into?" I asked.

"A new showroom and headquarters. The company outgrew the last office and gallery. Since I had to move, I decided to relocate to a city that would provide easier access."

"What does Walden Inc. do?" It had nothing to do with the investigation, but inquiring minds wanted to know.

"The company deals in lumber and fur."

The mention of those two resources immediately triggered my defenses. I blinked but didn't panic. Despite his company's products, the man didn't wear plaid or carry an axe or rifle like most huntsman did. In fact, in his tailored suit, Walden looked very much unlike someone who made a living out in the wild. More like a businessman who presided at the top of a company, making money off the hard work of others. "That seems an odd combination."

"Not to my family. We've been selling our products for more than fifty years," Walden boasted.

"It must be lucrative to be able to afford a place like this." It slipped out, but he didn't take offense.

"Very. It should be noted, when I say lumber, I don't mean the regular kind you can buy in a big box store but the harder-to-get stuff. It's amazing what people will pay for exotic wood."

"And the fur?"

"Again, nothing mass-produced."

"What kind of animals?"

"Depends on the menace." He spread his hands. "While the bigger cities are lucky to have a bureau to handle certain threats, more remote places aren't as fortunate and will hire the services of those who can provide aid."

"You kill monsters." I didn't actually care if he did. Someone had to do it. Heck, I'd done it. But to build a business around it?

"I hunt down those threatening, yes, and I don't take a fee, just the remains, which are then repurposed. Restaurants dealing in rarities buy the meat. The bones are usually snatched up by apothecaries, while the fur and skin become clothing or, if large enough, a blanket or rug."

He made it sound altruistic. Me, I felt stupid for not knowing there even existed a market for those types of things. "When you say you hunt down, do you mean you have a team that you send out to do it?"

"I am the one taking the creature's life. It would be remiss of me to ask someone else to put themselves in danger."

My witness claimed to be more than just a businessman in a suit but did that make him a true huntsman? Could be he exaggerated about his involvement in the hunt. "Do you have these types of missions often?"

His shoulders rolled. "Depends. Some months, I might have two or three but then go stretches with nothing."

A one-man hunting party that goes months without a job? "Doesn't seem like steady income you can rely on."

"Actually, the scarcity raises the price." He swept a hand. "Here I am being rude, keeping you standing. Come. I've got chairs and coffee this way."

He led me around the elevator, and finally I saw signs of an actual business. Or at least use of the space. A few tables were set up with tile samples and paint chips. Another held the aforementioned blueprint. A series of club chairs surrounded a glass coffee table and, near that, a coffee machine and a bar fridge.

"How long before this is all done?" I spoke to Walden's back as he poured us each a mug of coffee.

"Bert, my contractor, says it won't be more than a few weeks. We don't need to run much wiring, and we're leaving most of the space open." Walden handed me my mug, the coffee dark and aromatic.

Hoping to catch him off guard, I said, "Where's your dog?"

Without missing a beat, he replied, "Daycare. While he is well-behaved if left alone, given I put in full days, I don't want him neglected. Why?"

No point in hiding. "I swung by your house and didn't hear any barking."

"Even when home, Rambo isn't usually noisy." He seemed unbothered by the news that I'd been there, though he did ask, "Were you wanting to follow up on yesterday's events?"

I nodded. "I don't suppose you happened to remember any new details. Even the slightest thing could make a difference."

Walden frowned. "I've racked my brain, but I honestly don't think I forgot anything."

More reason to doubt his professional claims. Huntsmen couldn't be successful without being observant. A true hunter would notice every single detail around him, from the bend of a branch to the faintest impression on the ground. This guy had given us no more information than any other civvy who might have happened upon the site.

"You say you were walking when Rambo ran into the woods. Did you see any vehicles parked nearby?" If he didn't have any new details to offer, it was up to me to try to come up with something we hadn't already asked him.

"There's always cars parked," he remarked.

"What about one that seemed out of place? I mean, if you do that route often, you most likely know what to expect."

He snapped his fingers. "Now that you mention it, there was a rather battered truck parked opposite the park. It only struck me because the vehicles in the neighborhood tend to be less decrepit."

"Do you know the make and model? The color?"

"It was black with rust on the panels above the tires. As to what type?" He shrugged. "I wasn't paying attention."

A shame because that vague of a description didn't help much. "Anything else? Someone else walking? Maybe a sound."

"As I told the cops yesterday, no. I tend to mind my business." He looked chagrinned.

"It's okay. It's just always worth asking again, just in case a witness remembers more once the shock wears off."

"Sorry. I wish I had more to tell you."

I nodded and pivoted the questioning, directly addressing what I'd been wondering since I'd found out his profession. "If you regularly hunt down monsters, you must be used to seeing this kind of carnage."

Walden grimaced. "No, actually. I'm usually called

in after a threat has been identified. I just go in to take them out and there's never any reason for me to examine their victims. Not to mention, I've never heard of this level of slaughter."

"Right." He could be telling the truth, but something wasn't adding up. This large, expensive office space, his admitting he only had occasional hunting jobs, plus the fact that he'd been so shaken up at the scene... No way was he a huntsman, just a pretentious rich guy who liked to pretend he was tough.

"I'm a little shook, to be honest. To think this was happening in my neighborhood..." He ducked his head.

"I'm sure we'll capture whoever or whatever it is soon."

"I hope so. I'd hate for someone else to die so horribly. Torn apart like that. What kind of savage beast would do such a thing?"

An odd thing for a self-proclaimed monster hunter to remark, especially given he'd claimed to see a wolf.

"Don't confront," I ordered sternly, not wanting pretty boy to find out the hard way how vicious a beast could really be. "You said yourself, the Grimm monsters don't usually behave like this. We don't know what we're dealing with, so if you see if you see anything out of the ordinary, call the bureau for assistance."

"Of course." Said with an ease and a blank face that I couldn't read. Was Walden planning to put on his fancy hunting duds and head out into the woods himself, or was he smart enough to be scared into remaining inside, safely away from our predator?

Hopefully, for his sake, it was the second.

I rose from my seat. "Thank you for your time, Mr. Walden. I'll let you get back to work."

"Please, call me Alistair."

I didn't offer him the courtesy of my first name, mostly to keep the professional line. "Enjoy your day, Alistair, and if you do remember anything, even the tiniest of details, be sure to give me a shout."

"Will do, Agent Hood. And if you need anything, at all, be sure to pop by. I'm usually here in the daytime and home by six, at the latest."

After I left his office building, I went to the bureau and did some digging. Walden Inc. did indeed deal in rare items. When he said lumber, it actually meant deadfall harvesting from Grimm-Effect-induced forests. No wonder he called it lucrative. The cutting of the trees in these magical forests had been forbidden around the world because of the consequences. The most striking example being in the town of Redwood. People, frightened by the changes in their neighborhood, had tried bulldozing a copse that appeared overnight. The next day, the town had been swallowed by a massive forest. Entire homes, the inhabitants, cars, everything gone, and in its place a forest to rival the Black one in Germany.

So no cutting live trees, but deadfall appeared to be

okay to salvage, while also rare enough to raise the demand by the elite who wanted a piece of an enchanted forest in their home.

The company didn't just source the wood; they also built with it. The site featured images of homes with wood accent walls. Furniture. Even sculptures using knobby knolls.

Cinder leaned over me and muttered, "That is creepy."

"What is?" Because the current piece of art on my screen, a carefully carved wood nymph, appeared quite spectacular.

"Who would want any wood from those spooky forests in their house? It's like inviting the curse inside."

"I don't think the Grimm Effect cares if it has an invite."

"Still, it's like poking the ogre. No way. Not happening," she stated.

"You think that's bad, check out what else they do." I flipped to images of the fur and skin stretched into a lampshade, a coat of Yeti fur—which weren't the nice cartoon kind we knew from Christmas. The Yeti weren't a product of the Grimm Effect. By all accounts, they'd always existed, but with the advent of magic, they suddenly started making documented appearances, which usually involved rampaging through small villages and killing everyone.

"I can't believe people will pay ten thousand dollars for a wolf rug," Cinder murmured.

"Not just any wolf rug. Those transformed by the curse." Which technically made Walden a murderer. After all, the wolves used to be people in some cases. But at the same time, the bureau did tend to kill rabid wolves on sight. Turned out reasoning with them didn't work, and it took only a few agents being mauled to death before the capture policy changed.

"Even creepier," Cinder insisted, before grabbing my shoulder. "Wait, does this make him a huntsman?"

"Absolutely not," I assured her. "He's way too wigged out about what he witnessed and about the possibility of there being a rampaging animal around. He's definitely not the huntsman type, despite what he might claim."

"And what did he claim?" Despite my insistence, Cinder looked worried.

"He says he goes out and kills the animals himself, but there's no way. Guaranteed that if he does shoot anything, it's some kind of managed trophy hunt." I shrugged it off.

"I don't know—"

"Any word yet on forensics?" I cut her off, knowing Cinder tended to stay on top of those kinds of things.

"No. And yet we should have gotten something by now."

I turned in my chair. "Should I give them a shout?"

Before Cinder could reply, Sally from across the room exclaimed, "Holy schizzle on a stick, the lab is on fire."

"What lab?" I dumbly said.

"*The* lab. The one that processes all the crime scenes in the city," Sally explained.

"How bad is it? Did they manage to protect the samples?" Because I really hoped for a clue from them to help me with my case.

"Sorry, Hood. Reports are saying it's a complete and utter loss."

Well fuck. There went all my evidence.

5

Losing all the forensics sucked. I wasn't just talking about fluids from the bodies and the sweepings they'd gathered from the hut. The clothes the victims wore were also gone, along with the corpses because the lab housed the morgue in the basement. Double whammy meant we had nothing.

And a killer still roamed.

How could I investigate a case without an iota of evidence?

I left work in a less than pleasant mood. How should I proceed? The few names we'd managed to match to victims didn't help much. Belle had gone to talk to the families and friends while I'd been out with Walden. Unlike me, she had a knack for being sweet and compassionate. Upon her return, she had little to tell. Apparently, the ones we'd identified had disappeared suddenly. On the way home from work, the grocery store, or while out on a jog. No one saw a thing. No one knew what happened, just that they were gone.

Cinder promised to keep looking for a link between the victims, but I wouldn't hold my breath. My gut insisted they'd been chosen at random. Or if not at random, because they wore red. Red being the deciding factor.

Red being the color most predominant in my curse. Could it be a confused wolf, looking for his Red Cap and snatching anyone wearing the right shade?

Was the curse plaguing someone else, or could it be possible that it really was targeting me for a second go-round? Either way, I was determined to stop the perpetrator before the next tragedy.

I never even realized I'd picked a destination when I took off until I slowed to a stop by Regent Park. As gloomy as I recalled. Empty too. No one parked on either side of the road or in the small lot. The sidewalk remained empty. I would imagine once people heard of the massacre they went out of their way to avoid it.

It wouldn't last. People forgot. Or morbid curiosity had them seeking a thrill.

I left my helmet on my bike seat and hiked into the forest, the air changing temperature the moment I entered. Cooler, moist, the scent of decay predominant, that of foliage decomposing and not flesh.

Not a bird chirped. Not an insect hummed. Eerie, especially since the branches remained still as well.

Almost as if time had stopped. Wouldn't surprise me if it had. The Grimm Effect could do so many things once thought impossible.

The clearing happened suddenly, sending me stumbling from the forest into the open space. For a second, I thought I'd wandered in the wrong direction, for the expected hut didn't appear. Instead, tumbled and charred wood already covered in moss filled the spot where it used to stand.

Had I found a different shack? As I neared the ruined mound, I crouched and picked up a lonely latex glove, the kind used to avoid contaminating evidence when collected.

I'd found the right place, and any hope of re-scraping the crime scene for evidence was dashed. Grimm Effect or arson? Given what happened at the lab I leaned to the latter. Someone tried to cover their tracks. The killer most likely. A murderer who had just proven themselves cognizant of their actions. But more worrisome, now that they'd lost their spot for stashing bodies, where would they hide them next? Someone who killed that many in such a short time frame would not simply stop.

I did a walkaround of the clearing, head down, looking for clues as to what might have happened. However, the many tracks from the police the day before made it impossible to spot any new ones. Nor did I find anything other than the glove.

Fuck.

I stalked from the forest, and once I exited and my cell signal resumed—because for some reason it didn't work within—I fired off a message to let the bureau know about the ruined crime scene. They'd most likely send someone down to document it, even if it would be a waste of time.

Oddly enough, I left feeling a little more positive than when I'd arrived. The person responsible had obviously been rattled by our discovery. Rattled people made mistakes, and once the bureau warned folks to avoid wearing red in public, the killer would become desperate.

And that would be where I'd spring my trap. An idea began to percolate, one that wouldn't be hard to implement, although it would bug me to no end. My mom, though, would be ecstatic.

Sure enough, when she answered the door and saw me, she beamed. "Baby girl! Back so soon. You must have smelled my beef stew."

I did now, and my nose twitched as my mouth watered. "I will have a bowl, but I'm actually here for another reason. Do you still have that red cape you made me?" My mom, being the crafty type, had sewn me one when I turned twenty-one. I'd given her an incredulous look at the time and snapped, "*Seriously, Mom? I am not wearing this.*"

"*But how will you find your huntsman?*" my mom had exclaimed.

"I told you before. I don't need a huntsman. I am perfectly fine being on my own."

Only after did I feel bad at having turned my mother's smile upside down. She meant well; however, she and I didn't see the curse the same. She assumed she'd messed up her chance at a happily-ever-after and seemed determined to force her perception of how it should happen on me.

Mom frowned at me and said, "You told me to burn the hood I made and that you'd rather make a deal with a wicked witch than ever give in to the fairy-archy."

I had. Still felt that way too. "I need it for a case." I gave her the truth so as to not get her hopes up.

Her eyes widened. "This is about those murders."

"Yes."

"You're going to dangle yourself as bait!" she yelled.

"Who's bait?" Grams appeared, wearing a sweater that hit her knees. Used to be Grandpa's and she never washed it, claiming it still smelled of him. And it did, if his scent was mint candies and Dove soap.

"The bureau will probably make an announcement shortly, so I guess it's okay to tell you. The serial killer appears to be targeting people wearing red. So avoid that color!" My stern warning.

"Shouldn't you follow that advice too?" my mom retorted.

"I really wish you'd stop forgetting that catching

evil-doers is my job. And, yes, sometimes it's dangerous, but someone has to protect the citizens of this city."

"Why does it have to be you?" Mom pouted.

"Because I'm damned good at it. Now where's the cape?"

"In your closet," Mom grumbled. "I'll fix you a bowl of stew while you fetch it and break my heart." Mom stomped off to the kitchen, and Grams tsked.

"Oh, you've done it now. She's going to be a wreck until this killer is caught."

"You don't seem too worried," I noted.

Grams snorted. "You're meaner than any wolf. Don't forget, I remember what you did to that boy in high school. And you've only gotten stronger since. I know you'll catch the bastard."

"Thanks, Grams." I kissed her cheek and murmured, "Don't you dare be wearing Grandpa's red hat or scarf, though, until I do."

"It's too hot for that. But you'd better have this case wrapped up before those brisk fall winds start blowing through."

"That's the plan."

I headed to my room, and in the back of my closet, wrapped in a clothes bag, I found the cape. The red a shade deeper than my hair, the velvety material sliding slickly through my fingers. I spun it and put it on, the fabric covering me from the shoulders down to almost my knees. The hood, when raised, covered my head and partially concealed my face. A glance in the mirror sent a shiver through me.

My, what big eyes you have.

The cloak got ripped off, and for a moment, I debated putting it back in the closet. Did I really want to risk antagonizing the Grimm curse?

What other choice did I have? If I didn't do this, then someone else might get caught in it.

I tucked the cape back into the garment bag and headed to the kitchen, where the warm bowl of stew did much to alleviate my trepidation.

My mom spoke way too brightly, of everything and nothing. Grams dropped a few sarcastic remarks. The mood was almost ruined when I suggested that perhaps they should take precautions and leave town for a little while. Both insisted that they were safe, then moved the conversation to other topics. I knew better than to argue, but I at least made them promise not to open the door to strangers.

By the time I left, I'd reverted to my unusual unflappable demeanor, but apparently, all it took was a swan to land in front of me at a red light for me to snap.

The gun came out, and I growled, "Don't even think of looking in my direction."

It wisely flew off. Then again, why wouldn't it? I wasn't a part of its story.

6

I pulled into the apartment building lot a second before another vehicle. As I removed my helmet and shook out my hair, I watched as the truck parked at the back.

My neighbor, of the ornery attitude, exited the dark old beater truck and dragged out a bag with a big box logo for a hardware store. No surprise the ride matched the man perfectly.

"How's the fix of the tub going?" I hollered.

He slammed the truck door shut before heading in my direction. "It's going."

"Meaning what?"

"Meaning there was more damage than expected. It will be at least another day."

"Another day!" I squeaked. "How am I supposed to wash my hair?"

"In the sink."

"That might work for your short locks, but this?" I grabbed a fist of red. "This needs a proper sluice."

"What do you want me to do about it?" he groused, stalking past me.

"I want to know how I'm supposed to shower. And don't tell me a hotel. I am not paying to bathe." Nor did I want to drive out to Mom's again. I snagged the garment bag and trotted after Aidan.

"Will you stop whining if I say you can use mine?"

"Yours?" It came out high-pitched. "Listen, if you think I'm getting naked in your place—"

"Slow down, Red. One, I have no interest in seeing you in the buff. You're not my type. Two, I would be far from that apartment. I'm not dumb enough to put myself in a situation where you can cry foul."

"Says the man who had no problem barging into my place."

"To do my job. You borrowing my shower is a favor. Take it or leave it. I really don't give a fuck." He entered the building with me on his heels.

"How do I know you don't have a spy camera?"

He whirled so fast I almost slammed into him. "Jeezus, Red, what kind of pervs are you used to dealing with?"

"I work for the bureau. I see more than most," I admitted.

"Well, I'm not one of those freaks," he growled. "So again, the offer is there. Just give me a heads-up and I'll clear out of the way."

He headed into the stairwell, and it must have seemed like I stalked him since I followed.

"Would in the next hour be okay?" I wanted to get into the office early tomorrow. Run my baiting plan by my boss then map out where I should be wandering based on where the known victims were last seen.

He glanced at me over his shoulder from the first landing. "Yeah. I just need fifteen minutes to move my tools out of the way."

I understood what he meant when, thirty minutes later, he let me in and himself out with a gruff, "I'll be at the bar down the street for the next hour."

"I'll only need ten minutes." Unlike some, I didn't fuck around when showering. Wet the body, shampoo the hair, rinse it, condition, and, while that cream sat in my hair, soap my bits, rinse, and done. I never understood how some people took so long to do such a simple thing.

"Whatever." He left on that brusque note.

I took a second to look around his place. Same layout as mine, but the décor differed. Leather couch and matching chair. Wooden coffee table. Big screen television and video game console. A peek at the games stacked beside it showed he played similar things to me. *Call of Duty*, *Halo*, and some kind of racing game. I wondered if I'd ever taken him out when playing online.

His kitchen didn't have dirty dishes piled in the sink, and the drying rack sat empty beside it. While I knew I shouldn't, I glanced in the fridge. He had beers in the door with condiments, a few take-out containers, and packages of ground beef. His freezer had ice cream and more frozen meat. I couldn't judge. I tended to be rather carnivore myself. On my way to the bathroom, I noticed his bedroom door closed, and while tempted to look inside, I refrained. I'd already snooped more than I should have. Blame my investigator side.

The tools he'd mentioned were stacked outside the bathroom, and walking into it, I immediately noticed the massive hole in the ceiling above the tub. Exposed ceiling joists, piping, and signs of moisture were evident but no mold thankfully. Despite the obvious work going on, the room seemed clean. A single toothbrush sat in the holder. Toothpaste and razor were neatly lined on the vanity counter. The shower held a single bottle. Being a guy, he had something that covered hair and body. Must be nice.

Before I did anything, I searched for a hidden camera. No matter what he claimed, I took no chance my naked bod would end up on his hard drive or the internet. I found nothing suspicious. Inside his cabinet, he had a backup bottle of all-purpose shampoo, toilet paper, and a new toothbrush in a package. The bare walls had no holes or pictures. The ventilation fan also proved to be camera-free when I removed the plastic cover.

Satisfied I wouldn't be spied on, I laid out my

toiletries on the tub edge. Not many. Shampoo, conditioner, soap. I piled my body and hair towel on the counter, and then I undressed, utterly self-conscious. It felt odd to be showering in someone else's place even if it looked identical to mine.

In the midst of rinsing the shampoo from my hair, a noise had me squinting. "That better not be you trying to scab a peek, Mr. Fixit," I grumbled, rinsing my eyes and face. A tug of the shower curtain showed the bathroom door still closed and locked.

Scritch.

The noise had me glancing overhead just in time for the rats!

They tumbled through the opening, landing in my hair, claws scratching as they fell, their tiny paws thrashing. I did a very girly shriek and jig in the tub as squirming bodies filled it. Alas the combination of water, soap, and slick fur led to me slipping and falling. My head slammed the edge of the tub and—

"Red! Red! Come on, wake up. Don't make me explain to someone why I've got a passed-out, naked woman in my bathroom."

I blinked to see Aidan, three blurry versions, hovering over me. I managed to mutter, "Rat."

He recoiled. "Whoa, don't be calling me a rat. I told you I'd be gone an hour. When I saw the bathroom door was locked and you didn't answer, I busted in to find you passed out in the tub."

I groaned as I pushed up from the wet porcelain. "I

didn't mean you were a rat. I meant I got attacked by some. They came out of the ceiling." I pointed.

He frowned. "Are you sure? Because there weren't any when I came inside."

"Well then they must have fled out another hole because I distinctly remember the little bastards falling on my head." Ugh. A glance at my body showed fewer red scratches than I would have expected.

"If you say so. Can you get up?"

"Yeah." Not entirely true. When I went to stand, a dizzy spell had me swaying, and only Aidan's arms around me kept me steady. While his chest felt nice, and he smelled even better, I couldn't help but be me.

"I knew you'd try and cop a look."

He snorted. "Ah yes, because an unconscious, snoring woman is so sexy."

"Hand me a towel."

"With pleasure." He whipped it around me before snapping, "Think you can handle the rest on your own?"

The room didn't spin, so I nodded. "I should be okay to get dressed."

"I'll be outside the door. Holler if you need help."

"What if I can't yell because I pass out?" my reply.

"If I hear a thump, I'll come back in."

That would work.

He exited, closing the door behind him, but it didn't latch, the cracked jamb showing he'd kicked in the panel instead of picking the lock. Had he panicked? He didn't seem the type.

I held on to the vanity and peered at myself in the mirror. My face remained surprisingly blemish-free. My soaking hair dripped down my spine. It went well with my clammy skin and pruned feet. The water must have kept running while I was slack-jawed and drooling.

Where had the rats gone, though? The door had been closed. Unless Aidan lied about seeing them, which made no sense.

I dressed, feeling steadier by the second, before dropping to glance behind the toilet and then under the vanity, where a three-inch gap kept it from sitting on the floor. The hole and chunks of plaster I could see at least gave me one answer. The rats had made a new exit.

I emerged to find Aidan leaning against his bedroom door.

"You're going to need to call an exterminator," I stated.

"You still going to keep with the rat story rather than admit you slipped and fell?"

"Look under your sink cabinet and tell me I imagined it."

I stepped aside so he could enter and crouch for a gander. He whistled. "Fuck me. Those bastards chewed their way into the wall."

"Told you."

He rose to his feet, lips pursed. "I'll handle it."

"Good. Although, keep in mind if a regular exterminator doesn't work, you might have to file a report with the bureau."

"Don't tell me they're the cursed kind?" he groaned.

"Couldn't tell, but given they poured out of a second-floor ceiling? Very possible since they usually prefer to be underground." I didn't add the fact they didn't gnaw on my unconscious body provided another clue they might be of the Grimm variety.

"I'll keep that in mind. You okay to get to your place?"

"If I wasn't, would you carry me?" I taunted.

"I am not throwing out my back for you."

"I am not heavy," I retorted, stung by his comment.

"Good for you. Still not doing it."

"I see chivalry skipped you when it got handed out."

"What is your problem with me, Red? You've done nothing but cop me attitude."

"I don't have a problem. What you've experienced is my shining personality. If you ask me, it resembles yours quite a bit."

For some reason that made him laugh, a deep chuckle that tightened the muscles in my lower belly. "Touché, Red. Guess I'm not the most personable guy."

"Nope, but I can't judge since I can be a bitch." I shrugged.

"That's kind of harsh."

"But true. I don't take shit. I do like to dish it, though."

He grinned. "Ditto." Then, to my surprise, he added, "Sorry if I came across like an asshole."

"Sorry I fucked up your ceiling." My friends would be shocked to hear me use the S word.

"Bah. Shit happens, although next time you have a clog, give me a shout."

"Will do. And thanks again for the use of your shower. Hope the door won't be too hard to fix."

"It won't take much to get it working right again."

Look at us making nice. "Guess I should go to my apartment."

"I'll walk you there."

"Afraid I won't make it?"

"Yeah."

I didn't argue. If I got dizzy and fell, who knew when I'd be found?

"Stairs or elevator?" he asked as we exited, my bag of stuff hanging from my shoulder.

"Usually stairs, but may be better if tonight I use that coffin on a pulley." I grimaced.

A snort escaped him. "And here I thought I was the only one who hated them."

"Never could stand elevators. It doesn't help how many movies I've seen with them plummeting."

What I could now add to my list of things to dislike about elevators? How the close proximity to a virile male made my womanly senses go haywire. I seriously had to stare at the buttons lest I look too lustily at him. Must be a side effect from smacking my head.

Ding. The elevator doors opened, and he watched from the opening as I made my way to my apartment. It felt so far away, especially with the pounding headache. But did he offer to help? Nope. He respected my wishes, and in truth, I didn't need him. I made it to my door all by myself, but what did it say about me, a strong independent woman, that, for once in my life, I would have liked to lean on someone?

My hand shook trying to use my key, and I muttered, "Fucking lock."

I didn't realize he'd closed the distance between us until he took the keys from me and unlocked the door. He held it open, preventing the pneumatic hinge from slamming it in my face. I entered my place and dropped my bag.

"You sure you'll be okay?"

I shrugged. "A few Tylenol and I'll be right as rain."

"You might have a concussion that needs checking out."

"I am not going to a hospital." Hated the places.

"What if your brain is bleeding or rattled?"

"Why, Aidan, are you trying to stick around so you can watch me sleep?"

"No!" His nostrils flared.

"Good. I'll be fine. Not my first blow to the head. Nor the hardest." I'd once been knocked out by a donkey and didn't wake up for almost an entire day.

His gaze strayed from me to the coat rack with the bright red cape I'd hung on it. "What the fuck is that?"

"An old souvenir from back in the day when the Little Red Cap curse thought it would get me."

"You beat it?" He sounded surprised.

"Hell yeah, I did. I told the big bad wolf to take a hike with a kick to the balls and then sent the huntsman packing too."

"Did the wolf end up going back to normal after?" he asked.

"I don't actually know." Said with a frown. "Most likely he did. His sole purpose was to eat me."

Aidan cleared his throat. "I should go."

"Okay. Thanks for the shower."

"No problem. Yours should be ready by tomorrow. Night, Red."

"Night." I shut the door and leaned against it. Wondering what the fuck just happened.

I'd flirted with the ornery neighbor.

And he flirted back.

Wait until I told the girls at the bureau.

Only it turned out I didn't have a chance.

We had another murder.

7

I ended up catching a ride with Belle to the crime scene, my head a little sore from my incident the previous night. I'd driven to the bureau on my bike and regretted it, almost wiping out twice.

My eyes remained closed as she drove, yet despite the insistent throbbing behind my eyelids, I asked questions. "Who called in the body?"

"Shopkeeper. He starts baking early and saw it the moment he arrived."

"Forced entry?"

"Yes. The perp covered the camera in the alley without being seen. Most likely by hugging the wall to reach it. Then they drilled through the lock."

"They came prepared to break in," I mused aloud. "Any clue as to why that particular shop?"

"You won't like it," Belle muttered.

"I don't like a lot of things."

"It's called Grandma's Sweets."

I managed to not groan. "Did the victim work there?"

"No. Although she might have visited, given it's close to her place of work."

"You mentioned something about the body being posed?" I happened to glance at Belle and saw her hands white-knuckling the steering wheel.

"The sicko slashed the poor girl's throat then lay her on the shop floor in a pool of her own blood. He grabbed a display basket from the window and filled it with goodies before wrapping her fingers around the handle and making them stick with some kind of adhesive."

"He glued her hand to it?" I couldn't hide my shocked exclamation.

"Yup. He also used a spatula to shape the puddle of blood so it looks like she's wearing a cape."

Next level depravity. "That's sick."

"You don't say," she huffed.

"Was she wearing red?" Given everything I'd heard so far, I already knew the answer.

"The picture I saw showed her in a red T-shirt."

"Dammit! I thought Hilda was going to put out a warning."

"She had a press conference scheduled for this morning. No one thought the killer would act so quickly."

"We're dealing with a psycho, though. Unpredictability is the whole name of the game."

Then again, not entirely unpredictable, we had someone targeting people wearing red, perverting the Red Cap curse.

The police cars and crime scene tape forced us to park a block away and walk over, pushing our way through the gawkers. Murder brought people out in droves, driven by morbid curiosity along with moral superiority at not being the victim.

We passed by the caution tape by flashing our badges. Patterson spotted us by the door to the bakery and waved us over.

I had my hands shoved in my pockets as I stopped a pace from him. "Hey, Chief. Heard it's an ugly one."

His jowly cheeks sagged more than usual. "She was just a kid. Turned twenty-one last month according to her driver's license."

"What do we know so far?" I asked, despite the recap I'd gotten on the way over. Belle took out her phone to take notes. We'd long ago ditched paper in an effort to save the planet. Ironic given the Grimm Effect seemed determined to pollute it with curses.

"Farrah Longley, age twenty-one, was on her way home from work." The chief pointed up the street. "Waitress for the Rockin' Ribs restaurant and bar."

"She live around here?"

Patterson shook his head. "The bus stop for the night route is a block past here. We figure the perp waited in an alley and grabbed her. I've got officers canvassing to see if anyone saw anything or caught her on camera. Also searching all the alleys to see if we can find any signs of struggle."

"Cause of death…" I knew but wanted to confirm.

"Throat slashed. She bled to death." The chief ducked his head. "Poor kid didn't stand a chance."

"Is the body still inside?"

"Yes. I thought you might want to see it before the coroner took it away."

Not really, but first impressions could make a difference and in-person beat a picture every day.

I glanced at Belle. "You coming in?"

She grimaced. "I'd rather not. You know I don't do well with violence." Unlike me, Belle avoided confrontation. She'd only come this time because she'd taken one look at me and said, *"You should be in bed."*

A bell jingled as I entered the bakery, the smell of goodies overwhelmed by the stench of death. The store had no chairs or tables, but a long glass-covered display case that acted as a counter ran almost the full length of one wall with shelves across from it on the other. I didn't pay it much mind. The floor, or what lay upon it, drew the eye—and twisted my stomach. Good thing I'd not eaten yet.

I ignored the officers suited up in white taking pictures and dusting for fingerprints; my eyes remained on the girl. Sprawled sideways, positioned as if she were skipping. Her hand glued to the basket full of muffins. The pool of blood that had been swirled to create a cape flowing at her back.

Utterly grotesque. But that wasn't the worst of it. The girl indeed wore a red shirt emblazoned with a company logo from her work, and she also had bright red hair. But something about her tresses seemed off. I crouched for a closer peek.

"See something?" Patterson had entered and stood at my back.

"You said you had a driver's license."

"Yes. Why?"

"Can I see it?" I didn't want to mention my hunch before I confirmed something.

Patterson muttered to someone, who popped out and returned with a sealed evidence bag. Patterson took it from the cop and then handed it to me. The driver's license picture sucked but clearly showed blonde hair. The description said blonde too.

I glanced at what I could see of the victim's scalp through the fiery-colored strands and muttered, "The killer dyed her hair."

"What?"

I pointed. "You can see the spots where the dye leached onto her forehead." A jagged red line. "It's also on her scalp." I glanced at Patterson. "Is it okay if I touch her hair?"

"Go ahead."

"Can I have a glove?" Someone handed me one, and once I had it on, I grabbed a tress and rubbed it between my fingers, the tips of them turned red immediately. "Fresh."

"Holy shit." Patterson blinked at me. "Why would he do that?"

Rather than spill my theory, I rose and snapped off the latex. "No idea, but we'll probably see it happening again with his next victim. You and the director need to put out a warning. No wearing red and people should stay inside at night. No roaming the streets if alone."

"That will cause panic," he remarked.

"Better panic than death." I emerged into bright sunshine, but it didn't warm the chill within.

Belle took one look and steered me away, murmuring, "You look like you've seen a ghost. What's wrong?"

"He dyed her hair red."

"Why?"

I turned a wry smile on her. "Because the killer is sending me a message."

8

When we arrived at the bureau, Hilda called us in for a briefing, and we told her what we knew so far. By the time we finished, Hilda leaned back in her seat looking pensive.

"This isn't good. We have no leads other than the fact the Red Cap curse is most likely involved."

"And the wolf might be targeting Blanche!" Belle exclaimed, using my real name instead of my nickname.

"It's just a possibility," I quickly interjected. "Let's not forget the first victims weren't handled in the same way."

"Our killer flew under the radar for those, though," Hilda stated. "Now that they've been outed, and their crimes being bandied far and wide, they appear to have stepped up their game. Most likely, they spotted you in some of the footage."

"How? I never did any interviews for the media," I argued.

"Yet, you ended up in a clip. A reporter caught you exiting the woods."

I grimaced. "Well, that sucks Rumple's balls."

Belle coughed. "Um, so about the press conference to warn the public..."

The reminder had Hilda looking grave. "It's scheduled for half an hour from now. Me and the chief will be advising folks to keep the red outfits in the closet, as well as suggesting those who must be out after dark only do so in a group. Given the victims have only been attacked when alone, we're hoping safety in numbers will keep people safe."

"We'll have to watch for vigilantes." The Grimm Effect tended to exacerbate the hero gene in some folks, making them more likely to grab a pitchfork—or a shovel—and handle matters on their own. For some reason it made me think of Alistair Walden in a plaid jacket and orange vest, wandering around the woods like Elmer Fudd. Ridiculous, of course.

"The chief will be making a strong statement about that. We've got a tip line set up and ready to go. Additionally, given the way the last murder scene appears to directly implicate you, Hood, you should think about bunking with your mom or someone else until the perp is caught."

The rebuttal came quickly. "I'd rather not."

"If they're targeting you—"

"Then let them. I was planning to dangle myself as bait anyhow."

"Excuse me? I don't think so," Hilda flatly stated.

"Why not? It would be the quickest way to draw them out."

"You're asking me to put you in the crosshairs of a killer."

"I already am," I argued. "Instead of waiting for them to strike, it makes sense to intentionally put me out there. That way we can control the situation and set a trap."

"Assuming they fall for it. What if you, wandering around all la-de-da, set off their danger radar and they spot the trap? What if they wait until you're alone and vulnerable?"

An incredulous noise escaped me. "I'm often alone, but vulnerable?" I patted my side. "My little friend begs to differ."

"You're not impervious to harm, Hood."

"I am, however, better equipped than most to handle it."

Her lips pinched. "I have to go, or I'll be late for the press conference, but this discussion isn't over. I don't want you to do anything without my say-so. Understood?"

Begrudgingly, I replied, "Yes, ma'am."

"Good. Now, go home and get some sleep. You look like shit."

My head kind of agreed, but a voicemail from a certain witness made me change my mind.

"Hi, Agent Hood. Sorry to bother, but you said to call if I remembered anything. I'm working from home today due to construction noise at the office if you want to swing by."

I wondered what he had to tell me. Belle saw me grabbing my helmet and barked, "Where do you think you're going?"

"Our witness left a message saying he might have a tidbit."

"So call him back."

"You know I prefer in-person." Facial expressions and body language could tell me a lot.

Belle shook a finger at me. "You shouldn't be driving!"

"How else am I supposed to travel?" I retorted.

"You're not. I'm taking you home like the boss said." She grabbed her keys and briefcase.

"I don't need you to drive me," I grumbled.

"Yeah, you do," Belle countered. She followed me to the stairs and kept haranguing me. "You should have called last night to tell us what happened. Cinder and I would have come over to keep you company."

"Watching me drool in my sleep would have been a waste of your time."

"Probably, but I would have done it. And before you say something snarky, we both know you'd do the same for me."

I would.

As we walked out of the bureau, I asked, "Are you still driving that deathtrap?"

"My car is perfectly fine."

"I'm pretty sure it would fit on the back of my bike." Belle's ecofriendly vehicle took the term compact to an extreme level.

"It's good for the environment," Belle protested. She and Cinder had bought the same model a year apart. I preferred my gas guzzling bike.

"But not for your health if anything bigger than a squirrel hits it."

"Oh shut up and get in."

I slid into the very tight passenger seat before clearing my throat to say, "I don't want to go home."

Belle slewed a glance for me as she pulled from the bureau parking lot. "You should have never come in today to start with. You should be in bed resting."

"We both know I'm not capable of that."

"Well, you're going to try."

"I can't. What if my witness has something that helps the case?"

"After I drop you off, I'll go talk to him," Belle stated exactly what I'd say if our roles were reserved. Only, this was me, and Mom always said stubborn should have been my middle name.

"I want to be there."

"Why?"

I shrugged. "He knows me."

"And?" When I couldn't give a reason why, she slapped the steering wheel. "Hold on. Is this the hot guy I saw on those clips from Regent Park? I see why you want to see him now."

"What? No. That has nothing to do with it."

"It's okay to be attracted."

"Not in this case. He's a witness to a crime," I reminded.

"Not really. He stumbled across a scene and maybe saw the tail of possibly a wolf. He's not really a witness to anything."

"He's connected to the case. It makes him off-limits." I took great care to never cross any lines, even ones I drew myself.

"Not once it's solved."

"I am not looking to hook up."

"Maybe you should."

"Meaning what?"

"Just that you're a beautiful and desirable woman. One who needs to get laid more than once every few years."

The image of a certain hot handyman passed through my mind and my lips twisted. "I hate dating."

"Only because you haven't met the right man."

Also because I held myself apart out of fear of accidentally giving in to the curse. Even if I had been attracted to Walden, his profession would have been enough to make me back off. Whether or not he really went into the woods and got his hands dirty, he represented a huntsman. A woodsman. No matter how you translated the story, he covered both bases and though I'd wanted to deny it at first, the latest body confirmed that we were dealing with the Little Red Cap curse. I had to be on alert. I wouldn't give in. Fuck the Grimm Effect.

Belle gave in and drove us to Walden's home. She pulled into the driveway behind the luxury sedan parked there, exited, and glanced around. "Nice neighborhood."

"Pretentious, you mean." My retort as I left the clown car.

"Nah, pretentious has massive space between the houses. These houses you can just barely stand between with arms outstretched, making this middle-class suburbs. A place where people raise their families."

"Not this guy. He's single with a dog." As I spoke, I noticed a neighbor outside. A woman weeded her garden across the street.

"Give me a second." I hiked over and cleared my throat. "Excuse me, ma'am?"

She turned to give me a suspicious glare. "Not interested.

"I'm not selling anything, ma'am. I'm with the Fairytale Bureau." I flashed my badge. "I'm part of the investigating team for the murders in Regent Park."

Her expression turned somber. "Such a horrible thing to happen and so close."

"Your neighbor, Mr. Walden—"

"Who?"

Her confusion led to me pointing. "The man who lives across the street."

"Oh, *him*." She sniffed.

"You've met."

"Not really. He's very standoffish. I've waved and said hello, but he doesn't ever respond."

Being antisocial myself, I didn't hold it against him. "But you've seen him around. Him and his dog?"

"Him yes, but I don't recall seeing a dog."

"Perhaps you've just missed him when he walks it in the evening."

"Maybe." She sounded doubtful. "I'm out here a lot and see him come home most days. As far as I know, he doesn't usually leave until the morning."

"Have you noticed any strangers in the neighborhood?"

She shook her head. "Maybe, but then again, I don't know everyone."

"What about a truck? Black with rust?"

"Not that I recall. Is it connected to the murders?"

"Possibly. If you do see one, try to discreetly get its license plate and give me a shout." I handed her my card.

"I hope you catch that sicko," she huffed.

"I plan to, ma'am."

As I turned to leave, the neighbor queried, "Is the man across the street a suspect?"

"No, ma'am. Just checking out his story."

A story that made less and less sense. Why would he fake having a dog? A dog that was in his arms when he answered the door to me and Belle.

If me bringing her rattled, or surprised, he didn't show it. "Welcome." His bright smile proved engaging. "I see you've brought backup."

"This is my coworker, Agent Boucher." I waved at Belle.

"Nice to meet you. Won't you come in?" He extended his arm, and we entered.

I don't know what I expected from his place but also wasn't surprised by the casual elegance of it. It also looked impeccable. No mess of shoes or even dirt. The main hall had a new-looking console table with a large metallic structure I assumed was a piece of art.

"Shall we sit in the living room?" He led the way with the pup into a room that could have been featured in a magazine. Cream-colored fabric couches with a patterned rug and wood accent furniture.

"Nice place," Belle remarked, taking a seat on the couch.

"I can't take credit. I hired someone to furnish it. Can I get you a beverage?"

"I'm fine." My pounding head wanted to get this over with. Maybe I should have let Belle handle it while I drowned my misery with pain meds and whiskey.

"Tea would be nice if you have some," Belle countered.

"Of course. I'll just be a moment." He set the dog down before heading toward what had to be the kitchen. I sat beside Belle and hissed, "Since when do we take drinks from strangers?"

"Since I figure you might want time to snoop."

I smiled wide and slid off the couch, putting my ass in the air as I raked my fingers on the carpet.

"What are you doing?" she hissed.

"Looking for hairs," I explained.

"I don't see any."

"Neither do I, which is odd given his dog." I eyed the fluffball who sat there doing nothing.

"Maybe he's a neat freak."

"Possible." I peeked under the couch. "Clean there too."

"No hair doesn't mean much. I'm not a dog expert, but I'm pretty sure most small pups are of the no-shed variety."

"All dogs shed. Some just shed less. Either way, I should be finding something."

"And this matters because..." Belle drawled.

"The neighbor said she's never seen him with a dog."

Belle stood up. "Cover me." Belle sauntered back to the main hall, and I kept eyeing the arch he'd gone through. I saw a dining room and, beyond it, the kitchen. Or at least cupboards and a counter.

When I saw him suddenly appear with a tray

holding a teapot and cups, along with a creamer and sugar bowl, I coughed. Hard.

Belle reappeared and held out her phone. "Sorry. Forgot it in the car."

Great excuse, not that Walden seemed to care.

He set the tray down and poured three cups. I eyed the dirty-looking water and muttered, "None for me, thanks."

"Are you sure? The tea is a special blend," Walden stated.

"I'm more of a coffee kind of gal." The darker the roast, the better.

"I can make you some."

I shook my head. Regretted it immediately as my head pounded. "No, I'm good. So, Mr. Walden—"

"Please, Alistair. Mr. Walden was my father."

"I feel the same way when people call me ma'am," Belle tittered.

I almost cast her an incredulous look. Belle did not simper or giggle. She tended to be no-nonsense, like me, just nicer about it.

"Alistair, you said you remembered something?"

"Yes. Your questioning me about any vehicles in the area led to me racking my brain about that old truck and any features that might have made it unique."

"And?"

"It had a sticker on the bumper. I didn't read it but remember the image. A skull set within an emblem."

"A skull sticker?" Not something I could run through a database but could come in handy if we honed in on a suspect.

"It's not much," he admitted.

"Oh, I'm sure that will be super helpful," Belle gushed. "Every clue counts in a case like this."

Usually when Belle spoke, men paid attention. Not Walden—excuse me, Alistair. He kept his gaze fixed on me. I didn't like it. Was the Grimm curse trying to force something?

At least it chose someone attractive. But still… I didn't feel anything for him. Not like the insta-lust I had for Aidan.

Which I also wouldn't act on.

I realized Alistair eyed me and went, "Um, sorry?"

"I asked if you'd made any progress yet on the case."

"I'm afraid I can't speak about it."

"Of course. Forgive my boldness in asking."

"Oh, it's okay," Belle gushed, despite my evil eye. "What she really means to say is we have nothing. Which isn't a real secret. Whoever this person is, they've done a good job covering their tracks."

"Seems that way."

Was that a dig? "Just so you know, the city is putting out an advisory that people avoid wearing red or being out alone at night."

Alistair whistled. "That sounds extreme. This killer really has the police chief rattled."

"It's better to be overly cautious when dealing with a psycho of this nature," Belle stated. "We will catch the person behind these crimes. Don't you worry."

"And if capture isn't possible, we'll shoot them." My addition. I watched Alistair closely, expecting a huntsman to express some sort respect or acknowledgement, of but he didn't flinch.

"When dealing with a rabid animal, sometimes execution is the only choice."

I glanced at his dog. "How long have you had Rambo?"

"Not long. I was lonely when I moved here. I happened to visit a shelter and found him. Or should I say, he found me." Sounded sweet and yet I didn't buy it.

Belle beamed. "I love animals. But hate cleaning all that hair. How do you keep your place so tidy?"

"Robot vacuums." He didn't even hesitate to reply. "I also have a cleaning service that comes once a week. I am a bit of a neat freak."

As he escorted us to the front door, I paused, acting like I was hesitant to reveal my next request.

"What is it?" he asked.

"I hate to mix business with pleasure," I crooned, forcing a small fake smile on my face. "But I took a look at your website, and, well, I was impressed. Do you have a trophy room here? I'd just love to see some of your work in person."

He shook his head. "Not here, no."

I blinked, feigning disappointment. "Well, what about your hunter's arsenal? All your weapons and such? I'm sure it must be pretty badass, considering what you do."

"I keep all that elsewhere." His eyes flicked to the side, suggesting he was lying. But why wouldn't he want to show me? Perhaps he was one of those who had a natural suspicion of law enforcement agents.

"Anyway, thanks for stopping by. You ladies seem like you're doing a great job. I just hope you catch him before he kills again."

We left, and when we got in the car and pulled away, I said, just as Belle did,

"Did you—"

"He said—"

We both paused, and she waited for me to say, "Walden called the perp a him."

"Which isn't suspicious necessarily. Most serial killers are male, and I don't think we've ever had a female wolf."

"True. Assuming it is a wolf. The coroner never did have a chance to finish the autopsy on those bodies."

"The newest victim should shed a light." It would be sent to another city for processing, so who knew when we'd get the results.

I changed tangent slightly. "It really bugs me that the neighbor didn't know he had a dog."

"Well, if he only walks it once a day, she might not have seen it."

"I've never seen a dog that just sits there. Aren't they usually fetching shit or trying to crawl into laps?" At least the ones I'd met behaved that way.

Belle put the signal to turn left. "It was odd. Almost as if it were drugged. Maybe it's just old."

"So old it went chasing rabbits in the woods, which is how Walden supposedly found the hut."

"You don't like him," Belle stated.

"It's not that I don't like him. There's just something off. I can't quite put my finger on it."

"I think you're just wigged out because he fits the role of huntsman."

"So he claims. I've yet to see any proof."

"Would it be so bad? He is good-looking, self-made, and in the story, the huntsman kills the wolf."

"In the original story, Red Cap and the huntsman don't end up a couple."

"We know the Grimm Effect has been taking liberties with the stories."

"Don't remind me." I drummed my fingers. "What were you looking for in the hall?"

"I peeked in the hall closet at his shoes."

"And?"

"None of them appeared dirty. So if he was the killer, he hid those shoes elsewhere or got rid of them."

"Hold on. You think he might be our guy?"

"I think there's something odd about the fellow. I

mean, on the surface, he seems great. Handsome, well off, polite, his home is lovely, but there's something about him—"

"That sets off the creep-dar." I nodded because I totally understood.

Despite my bike being parked at the bureau, Belle insisted on dropping me at the house, saying, "Cinder or I will grab you in the morning. And if we deem you fit, you can take it home tomorrow."

"Anyone ever tell you you're bossy?"

"All the time," she replied with a grin. "Want me to walk you upstairs?"

"No!"

"But you heard the boss. She doesn't want you alone or taking chances."

"It's the middle of the day. I'll be fine."

"If you're not, I will be pissed," Belle huffed.

"Love you too. Bye." I trudged into my building and, despite everyone treating me like an invalid, chose to use the stairs, clomping up them in my boots and regretting each vibrating step. But I made it, only to enter my apartment and realize I had company.

A rock song played softly on a mini speaker outside my bathroom. I peeked in to see an ass in the air. I almost slapped it. Instead, I leaned against the doorjamb.

"Does your being here mean my shower still isn't ready?"

He didn't turn to look. "Actually, I'm just about done. I'm seating the drain with putty."

"How long does it take to dry?"

"No time. Plumber's putty works instantly." He pushed up from the tub. "Voila. Your shower is ready to go."

"Really?" I couldn't help but smile at the news.

"All fixed but do me a favor, and no more plunging."

"Yes, sir." Then, because I remembered the mess in his bathroom, "How's the hole in your shower?"

"Still there, but that won't be a big deal to fix. I'll throw up some drywall, tape, and plaster. If you hear my sander going, don't freak out about the noise."

"Deal." Then I don't know why, but I said, "Hungry?"

His mouth rounded. "You're going to cook for me?"

"God, I would never inflict the torture of my cooking on you or anyone. I was talking more like ordering in some pizza. Think of it as a thank you and apology."

"I was just doing my job."

"And I was a bit of a bitch about it. So let me make it up to you. We can talk about *COD* and the new expansion pack."

His expression brightened. "You play?"

He'd obviously not rummaged through my things. "Yeah." And from there, we started actually chatting like two people. No verbal traps for him to fall into. No thinly veiled insults, unless ragging on game play counted. The pizza was perfect, meat lovers all the way.

When he grunted, "I should get going. It's late," I realized we'd spent the last four hours hanging out. I couldn't remember the last time I did that with someone outside of my usual circle of friends.

"This was fun," I stated awkwardly.

"It was," he agreed softly. He was standing at the door, his hand on the knob, when I impulsively threw myself at him. I wasn't the type to wait to be seduced.

I grabbed him by the face, pulled him down, and kissed him.

His lips were stiff at first then softened as he joined me in sliding and tasting lips.

It ended with him abruptly pulling away with a gruff, "Thanks for dinner."

He fled, leaving me bemused and horny.

Good thing I had a toy to fix that.

9

I felt better after a night's rest—and a battery-generated orgasm. The morning shower was even more amazing. By the time I'd dressed, Cinder buzzed me to say she was waiting downstairs.

I emerged to find her crouched on the sidewalk, talking to the asphalt. Not all that strange if you knew Cinder.

"Who you chatting with?" I questioned.

Cinder glanced at me over her shoulder and waved a hand. "Talking to the sewer rat."

I peered over her to see the tip of a pink nose. "And what's the rat saying?"

"A lot but I can't understand it. I think it's speaking German."

A strange rat in the wrong place? It reminded me of the incident the other night. "Could the Grimm Effect have relocated them?"

Cinder got pensive. "I mean it's possible. Its magic can do unpredictable things. But why would it move rats?"

"We've seen heroes and other main characters in curses travel great distances."

"Travel yes, but teleported from one place to another?" Cinder pursed her lips. "That would be new."

"We did talk about how the curse might be evolving."

"I think it's time to stop talking about and admit it is. I'll file a report about the rat. If the curse is starting to migrate players, then our job just got more difficult."

As we got into her car—the tiny death trap with its little engine, which most likely had a single hamster running in a wheel—I asked, "Anything new come in overnight?" I knew social media buzzed after the press conference. Citizens freaking out, *"Why aren't the police protecting us?" "Why is the bureau not handling this?" "OMG, I think I'm next." "I have to wear red, it makes my tits look great."*

"No. People must have actually listened. No new victims."

"That we know of." My ominous addition, which proved to be prophetic.

We entered the bureau to see Belle standing with the boss, hands gesturing wildly. When they beckoned me and Cinder, we hightailed it.

"What's up?" I asked.

"We have a new crime scene." Hilda's expression couldn't have been grimmer. "Two victims this time. A grandmother and her granddaughter."

"Two?" Cinder squeaked.

"Where?" I asked.

"Inside their home." Belle flashed a printed sheet at me. "The mother of the girl, one Nora Lennin, who is the daughter of the older woman, found them when she came off her nursing shift."

"How bad is it?" I readied myself and a good thing because the images hit hard. Like the bakery, the bodies had been posed. Grandmother killed in her bed, which didn't sound so strange until you added the fact she'd been dressed in a voluminous nightgown with matching cap and little spectacles perched on the tip of her nose. Not her usual attire or even something she owned according to the daughter's statement. As for the kid, only nineteen, she'd been dressed postmortem in a red hooded romper, had her hair dyed a brilliant crimson, and was posed with another goodie-filled basket.

Sick. Very sick. But odd too. Why pose them? In the story, the wolf swallowed grandma and Red Cap whole, forcing the huntsman to cut it open to rescue them. I'd thought the posed girl in the bakery might be a message to me, but I still hadn't come up with an explanation for why the killer had piled bodies in the hut. Perhaps we shouldn't blame the curse. Could be someone obsessed with the tale. I wouldn't know until I started investigating the new site.

"Where's the crime scene?" I asked. "I'll head over for a look."

Hilda shook her head. "Patterson said to not bother as they've already moved the bodies and are trying to keep it quiet to forestall any panic."

"Maybe people should panic," I muttered.

"Tell her the rest," Belle urged.

I didn't think Hilda could look grimmer. She proved me wrong. "Forensics came back from the bakery victim. Her throat was slashed by a claw. They also found a few strands of hair, canine in origin."

"Meaning it's definitely a wolf." I kind of figured, but having the evidence to back it up always helped. There went any hope of it being some kind of psycho deranged fan.

"It appears so."

"DNA is good. What name popped up when they ran it against the database?" With everyone on file, it should be—

"Unfortunately, the strands didn't have the necessary follicle for a proper test." Cinder pointed to her tablet, where she read the report as Hilda briefed us.

"That's bullshit," I exclaimed.

"Hopefully the new crime scene will have better evidence. Until we have a name, and given the way the perp is now murdering every night, the bureau sent a special team."

I arched a brow. "To do what? We're already working the case."

"You'll still be working it. This team is to track the wolf."

"Wait, are you talking about the Grimm Knights?" I'd heard of them but never had to deal with any. Like some in our office—such as Luanne—these were people caught by the curse, but in a good, not bad way. It turned them into heroes, the kind that thrived on tracking, hunting, and saving the world. Only used in situations where extreme force was deemed necessary.

"Given the violence of the crimes, we need all the bodies we can muster to capture the perpetrator."

"You mean kill," Cinder amended because the Knights only rarely brought their targets in alive.

"As if it deserves anything less," Belle huffed.

"I agree, but at the same time, we need to figure out how it strayed so hard from the story," Cinder interjected. "The wolf in Little Red Cap only threatened the girl and her family. There were no other victims. The fact this one not only murdered indiscriminately but so abundantly deserves to be studied."

"That, and why they moved and hoarded the corpses in the hut, and then started posing the victims' bodies after they lost the hut," I said, revealing the thoughts that had been running through my mind.

"Eliminating the wolf wouldn't allow us to study the behavior and figure out what's going on with the curse. How else can we ensure it won't happen again?" Cinder finished with emphasis, and we stared at her.

"I'm not sure we can," I stated sadly. "Not everything is because of the curse. Some people are just fucked. And could be, this time, the curse affected someone with preexisting sociopath tendencies, and morphed a serial killer into a wolf." I wasn't about to give this monster an excuse.

"Something's changing," Cinder insisted. "We need to figure out what it is and how to counter it."

"I plan to counter it by ridding the world of a psychopath." I ended that line of discussion by turning back to Hilda and asking, "When does the team arrive?"

"They're here." The boss pointed to the floor. "They're downstairs in the lunchroom going over the files. I take it you're feeling better?" Hilda aimed the latter part at me.

"Yeah."

"Good, because the leader is very interested in your offer to act as bait."

"Really?" I perked up. At least I wouldn't be shunted to the side.

"Yes really, meaning, Hood, you'll be working with them. Belle, you're going to canvas the latest neighborhood to find out if anyone saw anything."

She grimaced. "Aren't the cops already doing that?"

"They're stretched thin with this many crime

scenes, and we both know you're better at this type of thing." Belle had a way of getting people to spill things they didn't mean to.

"What about me?" Cinder asked.

"Patterson is sending over everything they've got from the double homicide. I want you to do your magic and yank a rabbit out of those notes."

"On it!" Cinder practically ran to her desk to start, whereas Belle sighed. "Guess I'm off to do the grunt work."

"Would you rather prance around, tempting a wolf?" I offered sweetly. Not that I wanted to swap jobs.

She scowled. "You can have the beast." Then more softly. "Be careful."

"Me?" I laughed. I still grinned as I walked into the lunchroom and beheld the assembled team. To my surprise, not all men. Female heroes tended to be rather rare. Blame the misogyny of the original tales.

A large man—and I mean massive, his shoulders practically burst the seams of his shirt—glanced over at me.

"You must be Agent Hood," he stated in a low timbre.

"I am."

"I'm Levi, and these are my team. Sully and Pike." A dark-skinned man waved, as did the blond fellow beside him. "As well as Hannah and Gerome." Then before I could ask, he added, "Yes, they're from the

Hansel and Gretel curse, and they defeated their witch. Now they're hunters."

"Wasn't there a movie about that years ago?"

"I wouldn't know," Levi muttered. "I don't do television or movies."

"Is this your whole team?"

"The others are recovering from our last mission. But five of us against a single target should be more than ample."

"Don't you mean six?" I pointedly asked. "Boss says you want to dangle me as bait since the wolf seems to have fixated on Red Cap."

"Only if you're okay with it. We don't need someone who will have hysterics and make the task more difficult."

I snorted. "I'm good. I already planned to use myself as the carrot."

"It will be dangerous," Levi warned.

"No shit. This fucker needs to be stopped."

"Glad to hear it. From what we've gleaned, the wolf seems to hit mostly at night. But the locations are varied." He indicated a map on the wall with pins showing the sites of the murders and also the home addresses of the victims we'd been able to identify, with strings to show the path the victims most likely took. No pattern emerged.

Hannah came close and cocked her head. "Seems most are a crime of circumstance. Wrong place, wrong color clothes."

"Except for the most recent one," Levi commented, jabbing his finger on a spot on the map. "The pair weren't wandering around outside."

"That we know of. The report wasn't clear on whether or not the perp broke in to assault them. Could be he followed the granddaughter home." It was only as Levi removed his digit that I frowned and leaned closer. "That's only a few blocks from my place." Which I noticed also had a pin.

"Could be he lurked hoping to see you."

"He should have knocked. I would have welcomed him with some lead."

Levi chuckled. "I can see why your director volunteered you. But if all goes well, you'll never shoot a single bullet. Taking down the wolf is our job."

"What's the plan?"

"Quite simply, you're going to make yourself look vulnerable and, of course, wear red."

"Me, vulnerable?" I snickered.

"How about making yourself available? You're going to pop out to run an errand tonight on foot." He tapped my pin on the map then slid his finger. "You'll walk to the corner store while we shadow you."

"And if the perp doesn't take the bait?"

"Then we keep sending you out until he does. At the same time, we'll be surveying the area. If the killer is stalking you, we'll spot him."

"You said he. I thought we didn't have a suspect."

"We don't, however, historically, it's almost always

male," Levi informed me. "Now on the off chance he decides to break into your apartment and wait for your return, he'll have a nasty surprise. Hannah will be stationed inside for the duration of the ops."

I grimaced. "I'm not the roommate type."

Levi crossed his arms. "It's for your safety."

"Can't we just put in cameras and motion detectors?"

"We could, but if the Grimm Effect is abetting the killer, then they will fail," Levi flatly stated.

I blinked at him. "Wait, has that been happening?"

"Yes. Modern technology is no match for a determined curse."

"Well shit."

"Yup."

The discussion afterwards devolved into what I should and shouldn't do.

I shouldn't tell anyone about the team.

Obviously.

I shouldn't go anywhere without notifying them.

Annoying.

Do, wear red and be visible.

I would keep to a normal schedule, AKA go to work then home. The only difference would be my evening jaunts to draw the killer out.

"For how long?" I asked after Levi finished ticking off his demands.

"Until he's caught."

Please let it be quick. I hated sharing my space.

I drove my bike home midafternoon, all too aware of the generic white car following me. Hannah had been dispatched earlier so that she could stealth her way inside.

Which explained why I arrived and found her holding Aidan at dagger point.

10

"Hannah, what the hell are you doing?" I barked, kicking my apartment door shut.

"Looks like I arrived just in time. I found this guy hiding in your bathroom," Hannah stated.

Aidan had his hands raised and appeared unamused. No shit. He had a dagger to his throat. "Not hiding," Aidan growled. "Looking for my flathead screwdriver."

"Sure, you were," Hannah drawled.

I stalked into the bathroom and glanced around before crouching to peek under the vanity. I emerged waving the tool. "Aidan isn't lying. He's the building maintenance guy. He was here the last two days fixing my shower."

My explanation didn't remove Hannah's scowl. "Are you sure that was true? Maybe he just claimed he had to do repairs to get into your place."

"Because I don't have better things to do than creep on women," Aidan drawled.

"The shower was leaking. I saw the damage myself," I explained.

"If you say so." She made it clear she remained suspicious. Hannah leaned away from Aidan, the dagger dropping to her side, but she remained alert.

"He's a good guy." Then to him. "Sorry about that. Hannah is a bit overzealous when it comes to looking after her friends."

"Does she always try to slice people without asking questions first?" He remained belligerent.

Hannah smirked. "Honey, I've killed more assholes than you could possibly imagine, sometimes just for looking at me wrong."

I rolled my eyes. "She's kidding." I lied. I didn't think she joked one bit. "You should probably go." I edged Aidan in the direction of the door.

As he hit the hall, I realized I still gripped his tool and not the fun one in his pants. "Here's the screwdriver." I slapped it into his hand.

He took it but eyed me warily. "Everything okay, Red?"

"Yeah. Hannah's just an old chum from my training days with the bureau. She's staying with me a few days. But we're keeping it on the down low on account of problems she's having with her ex. So if you could not mention it to anyone…"

"That would involve me talking to people and

then, for some reason, telling them your business, which isn't even my business. Sorry about being in your place without permission. I literally thought I'd be in there thirty seconds to grab the screwdriver and be gone with no one the wiser."

"Hannah's a little on edge, you know, given circumstances in the city."

His expression turned somber. "I can't believe we've got a serial killer running rampant."

"Hopefully not for long. The bureau is working hard to identify and capture the wolf."

His brow lifted. "So it's been confirmed it's a wolf? The speech the police chief gave today called the killer an unknown assailant."

"We only just got word that the hair on the scene was indeed from a canine breed, and since the Grimm Effect loves wolves…"

"I wouldn't say love. Seems to me, those who get turned get the raw end of the stick."

My brow creased. "How so?"

"Because everyone always assumes the wolf is bad."

"Well, in this case, he most definitely is. I've got more than a dozen bodies as proof. And more to come if I don't crack this case."

"Guess we won't be talking *COD* strategy tonight over Chinese food," he offered with a wry twist of his lips.

Wait, was he talking about a gaming date? And one that I totally would have enjoyed? "I have an errand to run later, but I'll be online after that if you wanna party up."

"I'd like that." He paused, then added, "Be safe, Red. City's a little dangerous right now."

Didn't I know it.

He leaned in to brush his lips against mine. It took me by surprise and also stole all thoughts of reply. Bemused, I watched his ass as he headed up the hall to the stairwell. Nice view. I reentered my apartment to find Hannah waiting.

"You and him an item?" she point-blank asked.

"No." Not entirely a lie. I wasn't sure at this point what to call us. We'd kissed. Barely. Would it go somewhere? Time would tell.

"He's hot in a rugged don't-give-a-fuck kind of way."

I tamped down the spurt of jealousy. "He's not bad."

She snorted. "Please. I could see you devouring him with your eyes."

Was I? "We only recently met."

"If it doesn't pan out, let me know. I'm always looking for no-strings stress relief."

I definitely had to clench my fists at that remark. "I'm more into the battery-operated kind. Less messy."

The remark had Hannah chuckling. "Those do work, but I'm a gal who likes the real deal. My biggest issue is I attract beta males because I intimidate the alpha type."

"They're not really alpha if they can't handle a strong woman." I understood where she came from. My at-times abrasive nature had scared off more than one dude.

"My friend Chloe says I just need to wait for the right guy. But it would help if the right guy would show the fuck up. But enough of that. Let's get back to the mission. Your windows should be secure enough. No exterior handholds to reach them, but I did lock them, so if they did try to enter, they'll have to break glass. Your door has a decent enough lock. Anyone picking or kicking it in will give us ample warning. Any issues I should know about, re the building or neighbors?"

"Rats."

She blinked. "You have a rodent problem?"

"Not sure." I explained the oddity that had occurred, and her lips thinned. "This isn't the first time something like this has happened."

"German rats pouring out of a ceiling?"

"No, the fact that things that belong in one place are showing up suddenly in others. And by suddenly, I mean blink of an eye."

It reminded me of what Cinder hypothesized. "The Grimm Effect is changing the rules."

"Did it ever have any to start with?" her dry response.

"Levi says you and your brother beat the curse."

"Gerome is not my brother, but yes, we did. We

were runaways who happened to both stumble across the witch around the same time. Although, instead of a candy house, she had a minivan and offered us hot food and a shower. Before you say it, I knew I was dumb for accepting the offer, but she looked like a suburban soccer mom. Nicely dressed. Frail seeming. A façade, of course. Soon as she got me in her house, she stuck me in a cage to fatten up. That's how I met Gerome. With his help, we managed to escape and rid the world of her evil ass."

"I thought the Hansel and Gretel curse was always about siblings."

"Like we just said, the Grimm Effect is changing and has been for longer than some realize."

"How long have you been part of the Knights?"

"A decade now. When we reported the witch's death to the bureau, they kept us in custody to study since, as you said, we weren't the traditional sibling pair. Given we had nowhere to go, they asked us if we'd like to work for them. We started out as office agents but eventually got reassigned when Levi put the team together."

"You think this plan will work?"

"Honestly? No. This wolf has shown himself to be smart. Smart enough to stay unseen. Smart enough to have killed all those folks without anyone noticing. Smart enough to taunt."

"Meaning he's going to see right through me prancing around and bide his time." My lips pursed.

"Most likely."

"Then why are we bothering?"

She shrugged. "Because Levi gives the orders, and honestly, what else can we do? If the killer is watching, then most likely he's going to wait for a moment when you're vulnerable. It could be while you're at work. Or visiting friends or family. Speaking of which, I hope they're taking precautions."

My lips turned down. "I tried talking my mom and grandma into taking a holiday from the city. They refused. Said the wolf wasn't interested in two old women."

"Have they not read the story?"

"That's exactly what I said but they insist they're safe since I beat the curse."

"That's only if it's not making another run at you. If the wolf is indeed fixated on you, your family could be in danger," Hannah pointed out.

"Yeah, well, I might have not told them about the killer possibly being obsessed with me. My mom already hates my job as it is. I didn't need to give her more ammo."

Hannah stared at me.

And kept staring.

I shifted uncomfortably. "Okay, I get it. I'll give them a shout and give them a few more details to light a fire under their asses."

A great plan that didn't work. Several minutes in and my mom still didn't grasp the severity of the situation. "Mom, you are not listening. The curse could be coming back for round two. That means the killer might come after you to get to me."

"I appreciate your concern, baby girl, but I'm fine. We promise to stay in at night, and I won't wear red."

"Mom, he broke into the last victims' house."

"In the city. We're far from there, baby girl. We'll be okay."

"Mom..." I growled, and she sighed.

"Since you're going to be so insistent, would you feel better if we took off to June's for a few days?"

"Yes." Was that so hard? I kept my exasperation in check. "Call me when you get there. I'll be up."

"We are not going tonight. It's much too dark to be driving. We'll leave first thing in the morning."

I hung up with a scowl, and Hannah snorted. "Damn. That was painful."

"No shit. But at least she agreed to go. In the morning."

"Don't worry. I texted the boss. He's sending Sully to watch their place in case the perp decides to go after them tonight instead of you or someone else."

"Thanks." That slightly reassured. "What time am I going for my jaunt?"

"Let's wait until dark. Say about nine? I see you've got something red to wear." Hannah pointed to the cape. "Way to not give in to stereotypes."

"My mom made it for me ages ago. She still believes Red Cap and the huntsman are meant to be together, even though her own huntsman abandoned her. She still thinks he'll come back someday."

"Some people prefer the hope of a happily ever after."

"This is beyond hope and right into stupidity. It's been decades."

"The curse doesn't care about time."

The curse also didn't care about anything except getting its pints in blood.

11

Nine o'clock rolled around, and I readied myself. Freshly washed hair brushed out smooth. Deodorant in case things got intense. Well-worn black jeans molded my ass, paired with my favorite shirt—which Mom liked to joke missed some material since it cropped above my naval. I wore my shitkickers, AKA combat boots with steel toes. The gun I tucked in the back of my waistband, hidden by my scarlet cape. To add to the look, I even put on some mascara and eyeliner. Resist that, wolf!

"How do I look?" I twirled for Hannah, the woman having grown on me in the hours we spent together. She'd been involved in some interesting cases, and we'd swapped stories, only to realize we were more alike than expected. Both overly confident, stubborn, and dedicated to our work with the bureau.

"You look good enough to eat," she declared, her humor as morbid as mine.

"Here's to hoping the wolf takes the bait."

"Depends on if this is a game for him. If it's about attention and the thrill of evading, then I expect we'll see more victims before he comes after you."

My mouth twisted. "Nice pep talk." Not that I disagreed. It sure did feel like this fucker toyed with us.

"Just keeping it real." Hannah rolled from the couch in a fluid motion as she rose to stretch. "Now, tell me, what's the plan?"

"Again?" I rolled my eyes. "Don't walk too slow because it will look like I'm deliberately baiting. Don't walk too fast either because my shadows need to keep up."

"If you move too quick, forcing them to break cover to keep up, they might get spotted."

"I know." I didn't roll my eyes, but jeezus, this wasn't my first operation.

"What else?"

"Don't act scared or too suspicious. Don't fart."

Her nose wrinkled. "I never said you couldn't pass gas."

"I added that one because a wolf has a sensitive sense of smell."

The comment curved Hannah's lips. "In that case, maybe an extra spritz of perfume. Got any eau de wet dog?"

"I ran out," my dry reply.

Hannah paced around me. "I am still debating whether the red cape is a little bit too much."

The remark had me whirling so it flared. "Oh, it is totally too much, but let's be honest, the wolf knows I'm on to him. Knows I'm looking. This is the red flag to a bull daring him to come after me, which is exactly what we want."

"True. At the same time, maybe it's too obvious."

"His victims have all worn red, and this is the only thing I own in this color."

"Your hair might be enough."

"Might be. But if you ask me, wearing this is an insult."

"How so?" Hannah asked.

"Because it's me saying come get me mother fucker. I'm not afraid, you piece of shit."

Laughter burst out of Hannah. "I swear we're related. Very well, keep the cape. Now, if you get worried at all—"

"Shoot the bastard and we'll sort out the paperwork later."

"I was going to say abort the mission by waving both arms in the air. That will let the Knights watching know you're getting cold feet."

"Ha. As if I'd ever be so cowardly." I snorted.

Hannah clasped my hand. "Girl after my own heart. Good luck."

"I think you mean good hunting."

With that, I left my apartment and skipped down

the steps, the cape fluttering with each bounce. I flounced out of my building, my step brisk but not too brisk, my gaze straight. A woman out for a stroll without a care in the world. Cocky and confident. Let the wolf see I didn't fear him.

If the Knights shadowed, they did so well enough that I never spotted them. I made it to the store, bought some goodies—chocolate bars, licorice, and chips—and with my bag in hand, I walked home. Each step made me more and more self-conscious. The hairs on the back of my neck lifted. I felt watched.

And not by kind eyes.

Did the killer stalk me? He must have done so from afar because I made it back with no problem.

Almost.

The swans landed out of nowhere, the flutter of their feathery wings my only warning.

The six of them surrounded me, but I didn't worry. I knew this story. The Six Swans, cursed by a wicked stepmother. They needed their sister to sew them special shirts under stringent conditions to replace the ones that transformed them.

"Hello, boys. If you're looking for your sister to unravel the curse, then you should visit the Fairytale Bureau. They can help you locate her and fulfill the terms that will free you."

The biggest swan shook its feathers, and the magic shirt that made it a bird fell to the ground, leaving her there in the buff. Yes, her. The curse had taken liberties again.

The woman, her hair a long platinum, her skin alabaster smooth, smiled. "Why would I want to get rid of the greatest thing to happen to us? We already killed our brother so he couldn't ruin this blessing."

The statement put me on guard. "Are you admitting to murder?"

"Who me?" She blinked not so innocently.

"What do you want?"

"You."

"Why? Because you've just made it clear you're not looking for help." And no way did they flock to me by chance.

"We're here to give you a message." As she said it, the other swans all shed their feathers and stood there in the nude. They could have been sextuplets with their matching hair and features. They varied only in size.

"What message? Who sent you?" I snapped, losing patience and a bit discomfited by the boobs and cooches surrounding me. Where were the fucking Knights? Then again, did I really have to worry about these slender birdbrains? I could probably take them in a fight.

"My what big eyes you have," purred the leader.

"All the better to see you with," chanted the others.

"My what creamy skin you have." The leader licked her lips.

"All the better for marking when I rake you," replied the others in tandem.

"My what red hair you have."

"All the better to hide the blood when I kill you," a statement followed by cackling laughter.

Someone else might have been spooked. Me? I lunged and grabbed the leader's feather shirt from the ground, leading her to hiss, "Give it back. That's mine."

"If you want it, then you'll answer some questions. Who gave you that message?"

"A man." Announced with a smirk.

"What man?" I growled. "Name. Description."

Before she could speak, a single gunshot took her in the head. Her sightless eyes were less horrifying than the blood spatter on my face.

Her companions panicked. Their shirts went back on blurringly fast. They became swans once more, lifting in a flutter of wings and feathers and plummeting just as quickly as the sniper took them out. Five bloody bodies lay on the ground, a circle of corpses around me that left me gaping. Bloody hell.

When Levi jogged in my direction, I snapped, "What the fuck? You killed them before I could find out who sent them." Although I had a pretty good idea. Mr. Wolf had found a new way to taunt me.

"Wasn't me or my team. Someone called in about a suspicious truck that matched the suspect vehicle a street over. It turned out to be a false flag, most likely so the killer could do this." Levi glared at the bodies as if they offended him.

"Distracted?" I planted my hands on my hips. "Your job was to shadow me to foil the killer, but instead, he not only knows about you now, but he also took out the six bird-brained morons he'd sent to deliver me a message."

"What kind of message?" Levi asked.

"The kind that says the killer is playing games."

And I didn't know the rules.

12

AFTER THE INCIDENT WITH THE SWANS, I didn't make it online to game that night. I wondered if Aidan thought I'd ghosted him. But there wasn't a thing I could do.

The police and bureau required briefing. Reports had to be written. The crime scene processed. A search conducted in the area to find the sniper—which failed. Whoever shot the swans had done so from the rooftop of a nearby building and fled well before any of the Knights arrived.

By the time I dragged my ass to my apartment, I just wanted to go to bed. But Hannah insisted on hearing the whole story since she'd remained behind, making sure the wolf didn't gain access to my place in my absence. At least with Hannah on duty, I knew no nasty surprises waited in my apartment.

Once I gave her the rundown, and she cursed her team for being fooled by the false report, I went to bed but didn't immediately sleep.

The taunting message bothered, as it just proved that not only did the wolf think this whole thing was a game. A sick and deadly one.

Shifting my thoughts away from the case led to me thinking of Aidan. He'd been a good sport about being held at knifepoint. Did he think I'd ditched him? Would he be pissed? I couldn't exactly call, as we'd not exchanged numbers, just *Call of Duty* gamer handles. Oh well, if I ran into him, I'd explain something came up with work. Either he'd be understanding and we'd play at a later date, or he'd be an ass, in which case he could take a flying leap. I kind of hoped for the former. It had been a while since any guy had caught my interest and held it.

The next day, I went to work, only to find a basket waiting for me at reception with Luanne.

"Someone's got a secret admirer," she crowed, pushing the plastic-wrapped gift toward me.

My pulse raced. The wrapping crinkled as I pried it open to see what lay inside. My stomach tightened at the sight of a chocolate-shaped swan. Nestled in the paper confetti at the bottom, a note, typewritten, no identifying marks. To read it, I grabbed it by a corner so as to not ruin any possible prints.

Dear Blanche, or should I say Red Riding Hood?

It won't be long until we meet. But until then, I hope you enjoyed my living art. Or would that be dead? I've almost perfected the final tableaux, the one you will feature in. You should be honored to know you will be my crowning opus. I know you're impatient to meet, and that will happen soon. I promise. Fear not or, even better, shake in your biker boots because no amount of Knights or anyone else for that matter will stand in my way when I come for you.

The Wolf

"Bad news?" Luanne asked, probably noticing how I turned pale.

"Who dropped this off?" I asked rather than reply.

"Some courier guy about a half-hour ago. Why?"

"It's a message from the killer," my somber response.

Luanne gasped. "Oh goodness."

Goodness indeed. Although I would have used a stronger word like fucking hell.

Despite doubting we'd get any DNA or prints, I fetched some gloves before carting the basket and its contents upstairs. I dumped it on Hilda's desk.

"What's this?" she asked.

"The killer sent me a present."

No surprise, the fact it had been delivered to the bureau caused quite the stir. As the basket got taken away to be dissected for evidence, we gathered in the briefing room to discuss it, a group that included, me, the boss, Cinder, Belle, and Levi.

Hilda led the meeting but had me stand up first to tell everyone about the events the night before, plus the taunt I'd received that morning.

Predictably, Cinder snapped, "How the heck did a sniper manage to get past the Knights?"

"They can't be everywhere at once," a more diplomatic Belle interjected.

"No, the agent is right. This is on me and my team. We allowed ourselves to be fooled by a diversion." Levi took responsibility.

"Someone needs to talk to the place that put together the basket and see if they can give a description," I noted. I doubted the delivery fellow would have seen the client.

Cinder spoke without lifting her head from her computer. "I'm texting the owner right now. He's the one who took the call and put it together. Says it was paid by credit card. A pay-as-you-go version so forget tracing it back to someone." Meaning the basket wouldn't give us any clues since the killer never touched it.

We moved on from my incident to other news. Turns out I wasn't the only one who had to deal with dead bodies the night before. We'd had another murder.

"The killer is getting brazen. Last night's attack"—which once more occurred inside someone's home—"involved three victims. A man dressed in plaid and given an axe. His daughter, laid out like she'd gone skipping with her goodies, and a grandmother, once more placed in a kerchief and gown."

Hilda let it sink in before barking, "Do we know how he got in?"

Cinder raised her hand. "The attacker used acid to burn the lock and entered while they slept. It's thought he drugged the father first, as the biggest threat. While the autopsy isn't complete, they did find a needle mark, indicating a possible injection of a sleeping agent. We're checking the other victims for similar marks."

I shook my head. "I don't think you'll find any. He thrives on fear."

Belle backed me up. "He's an attention-seeking whore. I think he likes the struggle before he overpowers them."

It was Levi who pointed out, "Are they struggling? From what I've read in the reports, they've yet to see any signs of a fight from any of the crime scenes."

"He's right. Nothing's been found under the fingernails," Cinder reminded.

"Which makes no sense," Belle interjected. "People are wired to fight if in danger. I'm thinking that they most likely knew the killer and never saw it coming."

"Even knowing them, they'd fight the minute he transformed," Levi argued. "No one is going to just stand there and get gutted by a wolf."

"Unless they're afraid," Cinder whispered. At the

silence that fell, Cinder ducked her head before adding, "It is possible to be so afraid you freeze. Even as you fear the outcome, your muscles are paralyzed, your voice stolen."

Her explanation led to Levi frowning. "A temporary thing. Most people will snap out of it and try to save themselves."

"Unless the curse is amplifying their emotions." Cinder boldly eyed him for a moment before blushing and turning her head.

"That's bullshit," I huffed. "Bad enough we have no control over being placed in a story, now you're saying it's actively suppressing natural instinct?"

"Hasn't that already been the case? Look at the men who suddenly leave their families to go on quests. The stepparents who suddenly vilify their stepchildren," Hilda reminded. "But those at least follow a predictable pattern. In this case, it seems as if the Grimm Effect wants this killer to sow chaos and misery."

"Which stops when we find the wolf." A simple answer from me and yet one we couldn't seem to achieve.

"I take it you've seen no one suspicious?" Hilda asked while knowing the reply.

Levi gave a shake of his head. "No one out of the ordinary. Just the residents or people who have business in the area."

"We need a clue," Hilda exclaimed, losing her legendary cool for a moment. "Surely he's made a mistake somewhere."

A few actually. We had claw marks. We had hair. We had a possible rusty truck with a skull sticker. No actual sightings or fingerprints. Nothing to actually recognize the perp. It didn't help that the wolf could be anyone. The wolf only transformed when he hunted. In his human body, he wouldn't look, sound, or smell anything but human.

The meeting broke up with us no further ahead, but according to Luanne, I had a visitor. Walden stood by the reception desk waiting for me.

I emerged with a frown. "Was there something wrong, Mr. Walden?"

"Alistair, remember?" he chided with a smile.

"Of course. Sorry, Alistair. How can I help you?"

"Rambo ran off into those darned woods again and found something. I wasn't sure if it might be important, so I thought I'd bring it in."

He pulled a plastic baggie from his jacket pocket, which he handed over. I eyed the keys within.

"These could belong to anyone," I remarked.

"Indeed, but given the current situation—"

I interrupted. "You were right to bring these to us. Never know. Maybe the killer got sloppy and dropped them. Thank you." I didn't mention the fact that the keys would be almost impossible to trace.

Despite me dismissing him, Walden didn't budge.

"Was there something else?" I tried to stem my impatience.

"I think I saw that truck drive by last night on the way back from my walk. It went too fast for me to grab my phone, but I managed to remember the last three letters on the license. F. M. J."

That was more promising than the keys. "Hold on, let me write that down."

Luanne handed me a pen and paper without asking. Alistair repeated the letters, and I jotted them down.

"Hope that helps, Agent Hood."

"Every bit does. Have a good day, Alistair."

"Stay safe, Agent."

He left, and I rolled my eyes.

"What's wrong?" Luanne leaned over her counter.

"I already know this is useless." I waved the sheet I'd torn off.

"Why?"

"All letters, no numbers."

"Unless it's a vanity plate," she reminded.

"Duh. I should have known that." Blame the stress of the last few days for my mind farting. "Good thinking."

Only, I couldn't check on it because the database was down for some emergency maintenance. The tech working on it spewed some gobbledygook that essentially amounted to the computer glitching. I took it as a sign to get out of the office.

I visited the newest crime scene, a nice house situated in midtown, so not cheap. The cops on site let me wander through, and I didn't notice much of interest until I was leaving. A can of paint sat by the front door, along with other supplies.

It made me think of something. I called Cinder once I exited the victim's house.

"Hey, do me a favor and pull up the crime scene photos from the first home invasion."

"Okay. What am I looking for?"

"Were there renovation supplies by any chance?"

"Hold on." Cinder hummed before exclaiming, "Yes there were."

"Not sure if it's a pattern yet, but this place also had work about to be done. I don't suppose you can dig to see if there was a contractor or handyman involved?"

"I'll see what I can find."

With Cinder hot on that trail, and me out of fresh ones, I headed home. As I parked, Aidan, who'd arrived seconds before me, exited his truck, and I waved.

He strutted for me, loose-hipped in snug jeans. "Hey, Red. I didn't see you online last night."

"Yeah, sorry about that. Work stuff came up."

"No worries. Everything okay?" he said and then

shook his head. "What am I saying? Of course it's not. I heard the killer struck again."

"It was pretty ugly, and it's going to keep happening if we don't crack this case. Thus far, it has us baffled. All kinds of tiny clues but nothing we can put together."

"Sounds like you need a break."

"I do," I sighed.

"Why not pop up later for a movie?" he offered.

I almost said no. After all, despite the note from the wolf indicating he knew we baited, Levi wanted me to do another after-dark walk to the store. "I'd like that, but I can't come over until about nine. Is that too late?"

"It's fine."

"What can I bring?"

"Sweets? I've got chips and popcorn, but if you've got a sugar craving, you're out of luck."

"I think I can cover that."

We'd reached the building, but he didn't go inside. "I've got to hit the basement and check on the water heater. 1D is complaining she's not getting any again."

"A plumber and a gigolo, a man of many talents."

He pursed his lips before shaking his head. "Guess I walked into that one."

"In my defense, yes you did. Guess, I'll see you later then." We hit that awkward moment where we had to split up, but neither of us moved.

Until I did. I leaned up on tiptoe to buss his cheek

and murmur, "Don't choose something good to watch."

Then I sauntered off, hoping he got the hint because I needed the stress relief. And more than that, wanted to get him out of my head and dreams and into my bed.

Or should I say pussy?

13

I prepared for my evening saunter a bit earlier than the previous evening, and Hannah noticed me raring to go.

"Someone's eager," she commented as I swung on my cape. "I thought you were of the opinion we wasted our time since the wolf's aware we're deliberately baiting him."

"I've got a movie date later with Aidan," I stated, trying to act cool, and yet my heart raced as if it were the first time a boy asked me out.

The reply arched her brow. "A movie date at a theater?"

"His place, actually."

Her lips pursed. "I don't know if that's a good idea. I'm supposed to be watching over you. Unless you were planning to bring me along."

And have her cock-blocking? Hell no. "Let's not

get crazy here. I'll be fine. The killer won't have a clue I'm there since I won't be leaving the building."

"What if he comes knocking at your stud's door?"

I snorted. "As if he'd knock. If he did show up, pretty sure Aidan and I can handle it. Or are you worried about being here alone if he shows up?"

"Ha. That would be the last mistake he made."

"Then no problem."

She didn't look entirely convinced, but she also didn't forbid me. "Go on your date. I'll let Gerome know, though. Knowing him, he'll stake out the stairwell. He's got this overprotective thing with me as if I actually was his little sister."

"At least he's got your back."

"Wish he'd get my front," she muttered.

Did I detect some pent-up sexual frustration? None of my business.

"I'm off. Feel free to play any of my games, but do me a favor and set up a new profile if you don't have a login."

"Afraid I'll mess up your stats?"

"Yes," I huffed with a chuckle.

I left the apartment, dressed once more in my red cape, and did my jaunt up the road. The prickling sensation at my nape let me know someone watched. Good guys or bad? Hard to tell. Even harder to act casual remembering the sniper of the night before. While my gut said the wolf would prefer a more personal killing, I couldn't help but wonder if a gunman had me in his sights. I'd hate to die so abruptly without even a chance to fight.

The night proved void of foot and even vehicular traffic, people obviously taking the warning to stay inside seriously. The almost unnatural calm led to me being startled when a stream of rats suddenly emerged from a sewer to flow across the street and down the next hole. Since they didn't swarm me, I kept walking.

As I passed an apartment building much like my own, someone leaned out of a window and tossed down a bundle of hair, the braid fat and tied at the end with a ribbon. A new Rapunzel. I made a note of the address so we could send someone around in the morning. Most likely another teen with a mom who wouldn't let her go to a party. Fun fact, in most Rapunzel cases, the witch turned out to be just stern and overprotective parents.

I made it to the store unaccosted. As I exited laden with candy, three pigs trotted in front of me, and, yes, I blinked because pigs weren't in the original Grimm stories. More proof the Grimm Effect expanded? More worrisome, if they brought along their villain, we might have more than one wolf in the city. I fired off a text to Belle and Cinder, letting them know what I'd seen. We could deal with it tomorrow. I was getting laid tonight.

I hoped.

The attraction sure seemed to be there. But would Aidan follow through? I'd soon find out.

My step quickened as I spotted my building. Almost time and I had butterflies. A sudden prickle of my skin had me pausing to glance behind. I saw no one but felt eyes staring.

I gave whoever watched the finger.

Taunting? Yup. I was good with it.

I passed Gerome in the stairwell and wouldn't have even known he hid in the deep shadows, only he grunted in greeting as usual. He didn't talk much. To me at least.

As I reached Aidan's floor, I passed it to hit my apartment first.

A knife-wielding Hannah arched a brow when I walked in. "Back so soon? How disappointing for you."

"I haven't gone to Aidan's place yet. I wanted to change."

Hannah eyed me and my ass-kicking ensemble. "Probably a good idea since your current outfit screams 'I'm going to fuck you up.'"

An apt description considering the leather pants, shitkickers, and all.

"I got you some chocolate bars." I dumped out the stash on the counter for my temporary roommate with the sweet tooth.

"Ooh. Yummy."

As she went to scoop, I slapped my hand on the cherry licorice. "That's coming with me to Aidan's."

"Because nothing screams seduction like sucking something limp and red," she replied deadpan.

"It won't be limp for long." I winked, and she snickered.

I quickly changed, nothing fancy, because I refused to be anything but me. It meant soft track pants, a T-shirt, but no bra, and flip-flops.

Hannah eyed me up and down. "Way to make an effort."

"I'm not the girly type. So it's take me as I am," said as I tucked my gun into a holster and put it in a bag with the licorice. "I'll be back before midnight."

Her brow arched. "That quick?"

"It's been a while for me, so I doubt I'll need more than five minutes, to be honest," I stated, kind of shocked by my own brazenness. But true. It had been a long time since I'd been with someone, and the way Aidan got my libido running, I might come as soon as he touched me.

"If you're going to be later, let me know."

"Why? You going to barge in to check on me?"

"Yes."

"Good to know."

"Have fun."

I planned to.

With each step I took, the annoying butterflies in my stomach multiplied. Since when did I get nervous? Sure, I found Aidan sexy and, after our initial rough start, interesting. But why did my pulse flutter? I'd been with men before. Been on plenty of first dates, so why did this feel different?

Aidan opened the door before I could even knock, as if he'd been waiting.

"Hey," his low, rumbled greeting. He looked sexy and at ease in his athletic pants and form-fitting shirt. Ironic how we'd both dressed the same. I noticed he wore nothing on his feet, which were large—hopefully like something else on him.

"Hey." I suddenly found myself shy.

"I wasn't sure you'd come."

"Oh, I hope I do." Yup, it slipped out, and he didn't blush, but he did grin, a devasting thing to see since it popped the sexiest dimple. "I'll do my best."

If I'd worried about his lack of interest, that was dispelled the moment he dragged me into his arms and kicked the door shut.

He dipped his head to claim my lips. He coaxed them, teasing my bottom lip between his. He grunted as I clasped him tight, pressing my body firmly against his. My mouth pressed hard against his, and when his lips parted, I slipped him some tongue, a wet slide and rub that had me humming with need.

He crushed me closer, and I cursed the fact we still wore clothes. I wanted to feel his naked skin against mine. I dropped my bag of goodies onto a side table and grabbed at his shirt. He quickly grasped my intent, stripping it for me while I did the same.

"No bra?" He arched a brow and offered a small smile.

"I went for comfort."

"Sexy," he growled, dragging me back for another kiss.

Our lips meshed, and our breathing quickened. My hands tugged at his pants, pushing at them until he chuckled. "Slow down."

"Later. I've been thinking about this all day," I admitted.

"In that case..." He grabbed the waistband of my track pants and shoved them down past my ass.

I kicked them free and stood there naked, admiring him. Big all over. Big arms. Thick chest. Tapering waist. Muscled thighs. And yup, a fat cock.

"Before we play..." He snagged something from the table. A condom.

"Allow me." I ripped the box open and the wrapper crinkled as I removed it. He sucked in a breath as I rolled it over his shaft, stroking it as I encased it in protection. "Ready to go," I announced, staring at it.

It twitched as I kept staring.

"Fuck. It's like you want me to lose control."

"Please do."

With a growl of passion, he put his hands on my waist, lifted me off the floor, and leaned my back against the wall at just the right height.

Mmm.

My legs wrapped around his waist, pressing my wet

pussy against his cock, which got trapped between our bodies.

I did my best to grind against him, and he made a noise as he helped me by leaning his hips back enough that the tip of him could home in on its target.

He slid into me, the fit snug. I moaned as he kept pushing, slowly, stretching. I didn't even realize I dug my nails into his shoulders until he murmured, "Are you okay?"

"Hell yeah, I am." To prove it, I grabbed his lower lip for a nibble. Tugged it with my teeth while rolling my hips to seat him even deeper. I began to kiss and suck at his neck as he clenched my ass to hold me in place, his hips starting to move, the thrusts short but deep.

"Harder," I panted.

Aidan grunted and threw his head back, the cords in his neck tense. He began thrusting, in and out, fast, hard pumps that slammed his cock right into my sweet spot.

My pussy clenched around him, and all of me held on tight as I enjoyed the ride. He changed his angle slightly, and I shouted as he bumped my G-spot.

Over and over.

And I was done.

I came, loudly, tightly, insanely, the waves of pleasure just about killing me, and it kept going as he came, his cock pulsing inside the condom, thickening in that moment, triggering a second orgasm that left me weak.

A good thing he held me close, his face buried in my hair, because I was a limp noodle.

When he finally released me, I slid slowly down the wall and huffed, "Wow." I'd been with men. I'd had orgasms, but this... this took it next level.

It didn't end there. We made it to his bed for the next round, but any thoughts of cuddling and maybe dropping Hannah a line to say I'd be spending the night went out the window with a text from Belle just before midnight.

Meet me downstairs. The killer struck again.

14

NOTHING LIKE BEING ABRUPT WITH YOUR NEW lover.

"I've got to go." My naked ass rolled out of his bed.

"Duty calls?" He lay against the pillows, muscled upper body tempting me to ditch duty for fun.

I wanted nothing more than to crawl back into bed and lick those hard pecs. Instead, I turned away and left the room, hunting for my clothes. "Yeah. Our killer struck again."

"Again?" He didn't hide his shock as he followed me out of the bedroom.

"Apparently. Which is why I need to leave. Sorry. I don't mean to fuck and run." I didn't mention the fact my initial plan had me leaving early so as to not freak out Hannah. At the same time, had I not gotten the call, I might have extended my stay.

"Don't apologize for doing your job. Someone's got to catch that bastard. But promise you'll be careful," he growled as he stalked for me, so many inches of delicious man.

"Where's the fun in that?" I quipped, dragging on my pants as he pulled me close for a kiss. A nice kiss that had me tingling despite my many orgasms. "While I'd love a round three, I gotta go. I'll give you a holler tomorrow."

I left somewhat bemused, a little giddy, sated, and hungry all at once. You'd think the multiple orgasms would have solved that, but no. I still wanted Aidan.

Despite knowing Belle waited downstairs, I hit my place to change and advise Hannah of the change in plans.

"How was the *movie*?" Asked with finger quotes.

I blushed.

Me.

Shocking to anyone who knew me. I got over it and grinned. "Most excellent movie. So good we watched it twice."

"I'm impressed. Kind of jealous too. Maybe I should see if the handyman for my building is hot."

"Quickest way to meet him is to break something," I joked as I stomped to my room.

"Why don't you look like a woman who had fun, then?" she called out as changed into something a little more appropriate for field work.

"I did until I got a call that the wolf struck again. I'm heading out right now to the crime scene with Belle."

I skipped down the stairs and waved to Gerome as I passed. Got a grunt in return. I exited to find Belle and her deathtrap waiting.

The passenger seat remained as snug as I recalled.

Belle offered a wan smile. "Sorry to drag you out of bed. As on duty agent, the police contacted me claiming we had a Grimm crime scene, however, soon as I heard what they found, I knew it was linked to your case."

"Where did the killer strike this time?"

"Regent Park."

"The killer returned?" I'll admit to being shocked.

"Yes, and while the woman died, we finally got a victim who fought. Prelim report states she has traces of blood on her fingers."

"About time," I muttered. I'd been bothered by the fact we'd not seen any signs of violence in the other cases. I'd like to think that if confronted, even by a wolfman, I'd fight with my dying breath.

"Who found the body?" I half expected to hear Walden's name.

"Crime podcaster called Barry Grimes. He was doing a live broadcast about the Red Cap Murders when he stumbled across the body in the clearing where we found the first group of bodies. It's possible he interrupted the killer before he could finish."

"Holy shit. Have we confiscated his footage?"

"Yup. Cinder's in the office studying it to see if he happened to catch any vehicles parked or even perhaps the killer fleeing the scene."

The park loomed, especially ominous with all the flashing lights. I didn't really want to enter the gloomy forest but tramped along with Belle and Patterson, who'd spotted us the moment we arrived.

The clearing had bright portable lights set up to illuminate the area. The hut that once stood there was barely a mound under the moss that had crept over its remains. Quicker than normal but not so unexpected given the entire forest shouldn't exist.

The body lay sprawled, face down, blonde hair fanning the ground. The victim wore a red hooded sweatshirt and plaid cotton bottoms.

The sight of it had me muttering, "What happened to not wearing red when going out?"

Patterson cleared his throat. "She wasn't technically out. Appears she popped down to the basement of her building to do a load of laundry. Given the clothes strewn all over, the killer nabbed her there."

"And no one heard anything?"

"We're still canvassing the apartments, but so far, no one heard or saw a thing," Patterson noted.

I walked around the body and frowned. Why was she here? The killer had kept the latest victims near or at the location where they'd found them, yet they'd brought this one to Regent Park. Did it mean something?

I crouched and noticed the bagged hand. Blood stained the fingertips. "She fought," a low murmur that had Belle huffing, "Meaning the killer will have scratches."

"Lots of people have scratches, but here's to hoping we'll get a hit on the DNA. Who was she?" I asked no one in particular.

"One Jessica Lawson. Lives in that apartment with her grandmother."

"Someone checking on grandma?" I cast a sharp look over my shoulder at Patterson.

"The grandmother is fine. She left earlier that day to visit her sister. We've also done a wellness check on the boyfriend."

"He have any scratches on him?" I knew it was a long-shot, but figured I could ask.

"Negative. But the team did report back a description of him. The man's a park ranger. A big beefy guy with a full beard wearing flannel pajamas. All he was missing was an axe over his shoulder."

This was more than someone simply caught wearing red. "Meaning the killer specifically targeted her, trying to force her into a macabre version of the curse."

"Seems like," Patterson replied with a shrug. "This perp is getting more brazen. Breaking into homes. Killing daily. We have to stop him."

"I'm aware, trust me," I growled.

Belle dropped to her haunches by my side. "What's the end game?"

"My death?" I wasn't being sarcastic.

"No offense, but he could kill you anytime."

"The Knights—"

"Are only human and fallible. Let's be honest, if he truly wanted you dead, I don't think we'd be talking." Belle shook her head.

"Then how do you explain the red hair at the other scenes and the note with the gift basket?"

"Oh, I didn't say he wasn't taunting you. Just that I don't know if murdering you is his goal. This feels off somehow. Like there's a reason behind it."

"He's a psychopath. I don't think he needs a reason," my dry retort.

"Don't get me wrong. I think he's enjoying himself. The attention that sprang up after we found his stash of bodies is what I think led to him getting fancier."

"Fancy?" I made a moue of disgust at the word.

"Wrong word. I think he liked the reaction he got. Probably made him feel important. But at the same time, maybe he got offended by the headlines."

"What headlines?" I rose as I asked.

"The ones that called him a butcher, a psycho serial killer. It's as if he got offended and hence why he began posing the next victims. And look, it worked.

Now the headlines are calling him the Big Bad Wolf, the Red Cap Killer."

"Not exactly titles to aspire to."

"Because you're a normal person. He's not," she emphasized. "I'll bet he's got a huge ego and couldn't handle the way they denigrated his kills."

"Maybe, but how does that help us find him?"

"It doesn't. But at the same time, if he's looking for infamy, he won't stop and he'll likely get bolder and more creative."

"I wonder why he brought her here and didn't leave her in the laundry room. Or wait to kill her until she was back to her apartment, and pose her there."

"Maybe he felt nostalgic? Could be he planned to bring her here and pose her, then go back for grandma and the boyfriend, too, only the podcaster interrupted."

"What's so special about this place, though?" Before it became Regent Park, according to my mom, it used to be a farmer's field, full of cornstalks that, in the fall, the farmer mowed into a huge maze for people to run through. My mom was one of them. It was how she met my sperm donor. According to her, I was most likely conceived somewhere around here.

Blech.

The next hour I spent walking the crime scene, not finding anything. The first break in our case came when they moved the body into a bag to send to the morgue. In the spot where she lay, I spotted something.

"What's that?" I pointed to the black business card that barely showed against the dark ground.

A tech with gloves picked it up gingerly and placed it into a plastic bag before handing it over. Belle leaned over my shoulder as we read the card.

Looking for some help around the house? Plumbing, electrical, painting, and more. Call Dan the Handyman for a quote.

"This is it. We've got him!" I crowed.

"You can't be sure," Belle chided.

"The one thing those home invasions had in common was they were getting work done. Want to bet this is the fellow they hired?" I waved the card. "It would explain how he got in. Why he could get close enough to attack without them getting freaked and lashing out."

"Don't get too ahead of yourself. Let me send a pic to Cinder so she can trace who owns that number. Once we get a location, we'll head over to have a chat."

Would Belle look the other way if my fist did some of the talking with Dan? Actually, she might start hitting before I could.

"There's nothing left to do here. We should head to the bureau so we can help Cinder," I suggested.

"Only if we're grabbing coffee on the way."

"And donuts," I chirped. I needed the sugar rush

since there would be no sleep tonight. Not when we were finally closing in on the killer.

I could feel it.

As we drove away from the park, Cinder rang, and Belle's car answered, playing her call through the speakers.

"The card is a match!" she crowed before even saying hello. "Dan the Handyman is the guy who was doing work for those families."

"I knew it!" I crowed. "Do we have a name and address?"

"The number is registered as a business with a postal box, but it shouldn't be long before I track down who owns it. Thank goodness the databases are cooperating again." Cinder hummed, and I could hear her fingers clacking as she typed. "Jumping mice, you won't believe this. The partial plate Walden gave us? Guess who has a truck registered to that business with the license plate CQCFMJ?"

"Score!" Belle slapped the steering wheel. "About time. We've got him now."

While she celebrated and Cinder kept poking, I mulled the plate letters over. I didn't have my note on me, but it seemed like the last three were the ones Walden had given me.

"Okay, I've got a name," Cinder announced. "Dan the Handyman is owned and operated by one Aidan Malcolm, living at—"

"I know where he lives." My stomach sank. All of

me deflated as I realized the man I'd been falling for, the guy I just fucked, was a serial-killing wolf.

"What do you mean you know where he lives?" Belle glanced at me for a second, taking her eyes from the road.

"He's my building's maintenance guy." And then because I wouldn't be able to hide it... "And he also happens to be the guy I hooked up with earlier tonight."

Dead silence.

Cinder broke it first. "Oh, Blanche. I'm so sorry."

She was sorry? I'd fucked the serial killer—I'd fucked the wolf from my cursed story. Even worse, I enjoyed it!

Belle increased the speed in her little vroom-vroom, making that one hamster under the hood work hard to get us going. "I am going to bash his face in. If anyone asks, though, he tripped."

"I'm going to see if I can find out what food he hates and make sure they serve it to him in his cell!" Cinder huffed.

Sometimes it was nice having friends.

Despite almost being to the bureau, we rerouted for my apartment building. Much as I wanted—and didn't want—to confront Aidan, the Grimm Knights moved in fast for the arrest as soon as Cinder advised them of the identity of the killer.

Would Aidan give himself up or die rather than be captured? I couldn't have said in that moment which I preferred. I did know I hated him for lying, for being a psycho, but I also ached because I'd been falling for him. How could I not have seen the signs?

"You okay?" Belle asked softly.

"Not really." The honest truth. "He seemed like a decent guy. I mean ornery as fuck, but then again so am I. I would have never suspected." I shook my head.

"I'm sorry."

"So am I." My whispered response.

Before we turned onto my street, we got a text from Hannah.

Wolf in custody. Taking him to the bureau for processing.

I hated the relief that flooded me knowing he'd not been killed.

"Should we head to the office?" Belle queried, hearing the news.

I shook my head. "I want to be there when they search his apartment." See what kind of morbid evidence he'd held on to. What trophies he hid. As we pulled up, I was just in time to see Aiden emerging, hands cuffed in silver, ankles shackled, too, forcing him to shuffle.

Despite the flashing lights and Knights surrounding him, he still knew I'd arrived and turned his head as I exited the car.

His gaze caught mine, and my heart hurt. I also felt stupid. Stupid for not realizing the wolf had been seducing me the entire time as part of his sick game.

I turned away from Aidan and marched for the building, only to veer and head behind it to the parking lot.

"Where are you going?" Belle huffed as she trotted to keep up.

"To see something," I muttered.

His truck was parked in the back, reversed in so I couldn't see the license plate. I skirted it and stared at the license plate. CQCFMJ. Which in *Call of Duty* stood for Close Quarters Combat and Full Metal Jacket. Above his license plate, a sticker featuring the skull Walden had mentioned, which also happened to be the *COD* emblem.

Fuck me! Under my nose this entire time. He must have been laughing at me. Murdering people then weaseling his way into my affection. How could I have been so dense?

Belle put a hand on me. "You had no way of knowing."

"Didn't I?" I swept a hand to the truck and its plate. "I should have seen it. I'm supposed to be a fucking investigator."

"You don't expect that kind of thing from people close to you."

"We weren't close." We had only just started the process of getting to know each other. I knew he hated mushrooms on his pizza. Loved to eat chips while gaming. Hummed when he worshipped my body.

I closed my eyes and bent my head.

"You don't have to do this." Belle's soft suggestion had me snapping to attention.

"I'm fine. Let's go see what they found inside."

Hannah stood outside his apartment door when I reached it, as grim-faced as me.

She pursed her lips. "Sorry, Hood. My psycho radar must be on the fritz. I never once suspected him."

"Says the woman who had him at knife point?"

"But didn't gut him because, despite him being inside your place, he didn't give off a bad vibe."

"Yeah, well, guess he fooled us all." I moved from Hannah and glanced through his apartment, careful to not touch anything. Not that it mattered. The forensics team would find traces of me. On the wall. In his bed... Even in his bathroom from when I used it to shower.

What I didn't see? Any signs he'd killed anyone. I wore gloves to open the closet door for a peek. No bloody clothes or shoes. But then again, he'd have been the wolf when he killed. A sluice of his fur and the evidence would be washed away. Even if he'd dirtied his garments, he most likely ditched them, and good luck finding those. A guy doing construction probably hit the dump often with materials to get rid of.

Hannah poked her head in the bedroom, where I stared at the unkempt bed. The bed we'd lain in together.

"You sure you should be here?" she asked.

"I'm fine," my terse reply.

"You don't look fine."

I turned and pasted a fake bright smile on my face. "Couldn't be better. I mean look at the bright side. I foiled the curse. The wolf didn't get me."

And neither did the huntsman.

15

Rather than ride in Belle's car, I headed to the bureau on my bike. I wanted the freedom to take off at will. Not to mention I needed speed so I could race away from the turmoil churning within.

It didn't work.

I fucked the wolf.

Fucked a killer.

And God help me, I loved it.

Despite the crazy hour of not quite four a.m., pretty much everyone showed up with the exception of Luanne. Ralph, the night shift receptionist, greeted me as I entered.

"Hey, Hood. I hear we nabbed the Big Bad Wolf."

"Yup." A terse reply but all I could manage for the moment.

On the top floor, people were bustling. Cinder bent over her laptop. Belle had not arrived yet but only because I'd broken some speed limits. Sally waved her left hand as she talked to someone on the phone. I could see Hilda pacing in her office, her lips moving, and a stoic Levi nodding in reply.

Mahoney and Judd conversed together but stopped as I neared.

Judd gave me a small wave. "Hey, Hood."

"Boys." Slightly younger than me and usually a trio, which led to me asking, "Where's Tyrone?" He never missed a chance to be in on a big score.

"Down on second questioning the prisoner." Mahoney pointed to the floor.

"Oh." Guess someone had to do it and, rather obviously, it couldn't be me.

Mahoney hesitated before blurting out, "Dude's claiming he's innocent."

"Which is bullshit," Judd interjected. "He's a wolf."

"He admitted to being one?"

Both guys nodded. "Yeah, he came clean about that right away, but he's insisting he's being framed."

"He can claim all he wants. The evidence doesn't lie." And we now had enough circumstantial stuff to convict. Once the blood found on the fingers of the new victim got matched to him, it would be game over.

"Rumor has it you two were a thing," Mahoney dropped casually.

I could have been pissed someone spilled the news

so quick, but at the same time, I knew it would come out because I'd had to inform the techies dissecting his apartment.

"What can I say? I have shit taste in men." A bit of an insult to Mahoney, whom I'd gone out with on a single date. Not because he didn't try for a second. I just kept refusing. The man bored me to tears talking about himself. "Excuse me. I gotta check in with Cinder."

I sauntered to her desk, escaping from the uncomfortable questions and judgment that would arise from my brief affair with a serial killer.

I flopped into the seat across from her. "Hey."

"You look terrible," she claimed, lifting her head from her laptop screen.

My lips turned down. "You would, too, if you'd had my night."

"You couldn't have known." She tried soothing me.

"Feels like I should have, though. I'm supposed to be the agent who hunts monsters, and yet he flew right under my radar."

"He fooled everyone."

True, but it still stung. "Anything new since we last talked?"

"Actually, yes. A bag of bloody clothing was found in the basement of your building tucked behind the boiler."

"This just gets better and better," I muttered.

"Given the fluids on it are fairly fresh, we're assuming it's from the latest victim."

"Can you believe that prick has the nerve to claim he's being framed?" said with a bitter laugh.

"I heard."

"Like, for fuck's sake, we've got so much evidence. The wolf hair found at the crime scene. A partial license plate that matches his truck, even the fucking sticker on his bumper. Plus he had a connection to several of the victims through his handyman work. And now, the clothes he wore at the murder scene." I sighed. "What a clusterfuck." It made me nauseous to realize he'd killed someone before having sex with me.

"You forgot the keys," she murmured. "The set Walden turned in turned out to be a match for his apartment."

"Jeezus. How could I have played so easily into his hands?" It made me wonder now if the whole plumbing thing had been a sham. Maybe he'd wrecked his ceiling to get at my pipes to give himself a plausible reason to come knocking.

"The important thing is he was caught and you weren't harmed." Cinder reached over to put her hand over mine.

"I wasn't, but what about those other poor people?" I'd failed them.

"You tried your best. We all did."

By dawn, word leaked to the media that the killer had been caught. News channels didn't wait for an official statement and ran with the story. My mom texted to say she and Grams would be heading home since it was now safe. She hated being away for long, claiming her garden needed her.

Around seven a.m., Hilda emerged from her office to find me staring blankly into space and used a softer tone than usual to say, "You should go home."

"To do what? Wonder how I could be so dense?" I shook my head. "No thanks."

"He fooled everyone from the sounds of it," her understanding reply.

It didn't help. I stood abruptly. "Have the recovered clothing and other collected evidence been shipped off to the lab yet?"

Hilda shook her head. "We're waiting on a courier. Why?"

"Because I'd like to torture myself," my sarcastic reply.

Luckily, she didn't ask why I wanted to see the clothes. I couldn't stop wondering if they'd collected the same shirt he'd worn when we made the movie date with me earlier that day. He'd changed before I showed up. Showered too. Not suspicious on its own but with what I now knew...

The box with the things they'd grabbed from his apartment wasn't very big. They'd not really found much, if anything at all. Business cards that matched the one found at the most recent crime scene. Shoes that might have something stuck in the treads. And the bag with the clothing.

The generic and bland blue T-shirt at least wasn't the one I'd seen him wearing that afternoon when we'd made plans.

Hannah walked in as I frowned at the blood-stained fabric. "What are you doing here?"

"Something's wrong with this." I shook the plastic package. "The shirt is new."

"And?"

"I've never seen him wear anything that hasn't been well washed and worn." Could be he'd bought a throwaway set of clothing, but a normal person would have purchased and kept the new, not immediately ruined it. Disturbed, I began scrounging in the cupboards lining the wall.

"What are you looking for?" Hannah leaned against the table, arms crossed.

"Gloves. I want to check something." I couldn't have said what exactly in that moment, only that I wanted a better look.

Once I'd located the latex gloves and slipped on a pair, I unsealed the bag and withdrew the shirt, letting it hang from my grip.

My lips pursed.

"What's wrong?" Hannah queried, cocking her head.

"This shirt looks too small to fit him." I should know since I'd explored that wide chest.

Hannah grabbed her own set of gloves before reaching for the shirt.

"What are you doing?" I asked as she snatched it from me.

"Checking the size on the label because you're right. This shirt wouldn't have fit that beast."

I winced at the term. But it did technically fit. Aidan was a wolf. But was he *the* wolf? The piles of evidence sure seemed to point at him. So why did I have this nagging uncertainty?

"It's a large," Hannah declared. "And he's at least an XL, maybe even a double with those shoulders. I would know, seeing as how Gerome is close to the same size." She put the shirt back into the bag and snared the pants next. "Thirty-two waist. Kind of skinny for a guy his size."

"Maybe he wanted to throw us off track by using undersized clothes."

She snorted as she put the clothes back in the plastic. "Only if he wants attention. No way he could have buttoned these." She snapped off the gloves and began typing furiously on her phone.

"Who are you texting?" Nosy? Yes, but she seemed rather intent.

"Gerome is still at Aidan's apartment, inspecting it top to bottom for hidey holes. I'm going to have him check the closet for sizing." It didn't take long for Gerome to reply. Hannah glanced at me. "The shirts are all XXL, and the pants are a thirty-six."

"Maybe he lost weight since he bought those." I refused to allow myself any hope.

"Maybe. But something about this feels off." Hannah chewed the tip of her finger and stared at the bags.

"Given the blood hasn't dried yet, we're assuming this is from the newest victim, right?" I asked.

"Would seem most likely. Why?" she asked.

Rather than reply, I suddenly flew out of the room and went hunting for Cinder. She was at her desk as I rushed up to ask, "What time did the murder happen?"

"What?" She blinked at me as Hannah arrived on my heels.

"The woman we just found in the woods. What time approximately did she die?"

"We don't have the full autopsy yet, but given it appears the podcaster interrupted the suspect in the act, sometime around ten."

When Aidan and I were in bed. My mouth rounded. "Holy shit. It wasn't him."

"What do you mean it wasn't him? The evidence—"

"Must have been planted because I know for sure he didn't kill the woman in Regent Park because he was with me," I crowed.

Hannah muttered, "I'll be damned. He's actually being framed."

Hilda happened to be walking by and overhead.

"What are you two yapping about? Of course he did it."

I whirled to state, "Aidan couldn't have killed the woman in the woods because we were together at the time it happened. As in naked in his bed from nine p.m. until almost midnight when Belle called."

The sudden silence told me everyone had heard.

Hilda's brows shot into the stratosphere. "Are you giving him an alibi?"

"I am." My cheeks wanted to burn, but I kept my chin high.

"You better not be lying to save your lover," my boss growled.

"As if I'd do that," I huffed indignantly.

Hannah cleared her throat. "I can vouch she was gone for that period of time. And unless she managed to fly out a window, she and Aidan didn't leave that apartment. The Knights would have noticed."

"An alibi for this murder doesn't mean he's innocent of the rest," Hilda barked.

"No, but I think it casts enough doubt that we shouldn't railroad him so fast. The other evidence we found could have been easily stolen and planted. After all, as a Grimpher, he makes a good scape-wolf."

"Shit. Fuck. Goddammit." Hilda began to curse. "If he's innocent, then this is bad. So bad. The media has already announced we caught the killer."

"What if we haven't, though? What if he's telling the truth and he's not the wolf we're looking for? We have to warn the public the killer is still at large," I pointed out.

An unhappy boss rubbed her forehead. "Patterson is going to shit a brick." She stalked off, and Hannah patted me on the back. "She might not be happy, but in good news, our bad-guy-dar isn't broken."

Maybe not, but that meant the real killer remained a threat and would most likely strike again. But before I worried about that, I had to deal with something just as pressing.

"We need to release Aidan."

Cinder rose. "I'll get the paperwork started since they've already booked him." She put a hand on my arm. "Why don't you go see him?"

See him after believing the worst? "I doubt he'll want to even live in the same building as me after this." He'd hate me and with good reason. I sighed. "I need a smoke." I'd barely had any the past few days but could use that nicotine rush now. I headed outside and leaned against the building to puff on the stale cigarette I found in the pack kept in my desk drawer.

On my third drag, my phone rang. I glanced at the call display and frowned. I let it go to voicemail. I had no time or patience for Walden today.

It immediately rang again, this time showing my mother's number. I answered. "Hey, Mom."

"Hi, baby girl." Spoken without her usual exuberance.

"What's up? Have you left June's yet?"

"We got home a short time ago, but we're already wishing we'd stayed. Whatever you do, don't come here!" Mom yelled, and then a coldness spread through my veins as I heard a scuffle. Then a deep male voice came on the line.

"Good morning, Agent Hood."

"Walden? What are you doing at my mother's?" My heart began to race with fear and confusion.

"I thought we'd agreed on Alistair."

"Don't fuck with me. Put my mother back on the phone."

"I don't think so." A low drawl. "I think the time has come to finish the story, don't you?"

It hit me in that moment. "You're the killer."

"Give the agent a promotion!" he crowed. "Or not, seeing as how you so easily believed the false trail I set implicating that man in your building. How lucky for me to have a wolf so handily available to keep the heat off of me until I had all the pieces in place."

"What do you want?" I growled.

"To have a nice chat."

"Fine. Where do you want to meet?"

"How about the place it began?"

"What are you talking about?"

"The cottage, you dense twit. I'll be waiting with your mother and grandmother. Oh and, Hood, show up alone, or I won't be responsible for what happens to them."

He hung up, and I screamed as I tossed my phone.

It hit the ground and cracked. I didn't care. The killer had my family.

A mistake he'd soon regret.

A good thing I'd eschewed riding back to the bureau with Belle and had brought my bike. I didn't say anything to anyone. Couldn't. I had no doubt he'd kill them. Besides, he'd made this personal.

If he wanted to die by my hand, then so be it. He'd already twisted the Red Cap tale to suit his sadistic predilection. Time for me throw in my own addition. Screw taking goodies to grandma. I was bringing my gun and a thirst for vengeance.

16

The cottage looked quaint in the early morning light. Not even ten o'clock and it felt like the longest day ever. From the outside, everything appeared calm. Unlike my guts, which churned.

I left my bike behind Mom's car, leaning on its kickstand, my helmet on the seat. I stalked to the cottage, angry and afraid of what I'd find.

Walden appeared in the doorway but, for once, not in a suit. He wore a plaid shirt of dark green, blue, and black along with cargo pants. He leaned against the frame and smirked. "Hello, Agent Hood. So nice of you to come."

"Fuck you. Where's my mom and Grams?" I thought it encouraging I didn't see signs of blood. But knowing what he'd done to the others, I feared the worst.

"You can seem them in a moment. First, drop the gun."

I held out my arms and let my jacket gape wide open. "What gun?"

"Come now, Agent Hood. I'm not stupid. The one tucked in the back of your pants."

So much for going into this armed. I reached for my weapon, never removing my eyes from him. I'd only get one chance to drop him.

He drawled, "I should probably mention I'm holding a string attached to the trigger of the gun pointing at your mother's head. If you shoot me, she dies." He held up his hand, which indeed showed twine wrapped around his palm.

I bit back a growl of annoyance at him for figuring out my plan. Reaching behind, I pulled out my revolver and held it with a single finger before I crouched to place it on the ground.

"That's better. Now your phone."

"I don't have one on me."

"Bullshit," he snapped.

"It's the truth. After our phone call, it suffered a fatal fall."

He arched a brow, and his lips curved ever so slightly. "Temper, temper. Must be the red hair."

"Are you done being an asshole? I want to see my family."

"Of course. Come on in." He moved, and I

watched as he coiled the string around his hand to keep it from getting slack.

Holding tight to my anger and fear, I entered the cottage, which dared to appear homey and cheerful despite the calamity striking it. It should have been as dank and gloomy as my mood.

I found my mom and grandma in the living room, trussed with duct tape, their mouths covered, my mom's eyes wide and terrified. Grams, though, looked pissed. While her hair might be white now, she'd once been as redheaded as me.

The room had been tampered with. The knick-knacks I could have thrown removed. The coffee table shifted out of the way to accommodate the kitchen chair facing the couch, which held the aforementioned gun positioned on it, the string Walden held extending to its trigger in a loop that just needed a sharp tug to tighten and fire.

I'd have to do something about that before I took him out. What could I grab sharp enough to shear the tether without putting pressure?

As if sensing my direction of thought, Walden lifted his arm, pulling taut the string. "Don't even think about it. It would be a shame for you to ruin the final act."

"You've got me here. Now what?" I snapped.

"Sit with your family, as I have a story to tell."

A story? Like I wanted to listen to a bad guy's monologue. Then again, what choice did I have?

Hood's Caper

The sofa had room for me, so I sat between my mom and grandma, where at least I could shove the former to the side and take the bullet meant for her. This was my fault. My curse. I didn't want my mom to pay for it, even if I had to die.

Walden planted himself before us. "Once upon a time, there was a huntsman named Roland Chasseur."

Mom made a noise, and I froze in shock because I knew that name. I'd seen it listed on my birth certificate under father.

"You know my father?" I blurted out.

"Don't you mean *our* father?" he snidely replied.

My blood chilled. "We're related?" Gross on too many levels to count.

"Indeed we are, *sister*."

"I don't believe you. Your last name is Walden."

"It's my mother's maiden name. My grandfather insisted I change it when I went to live with him after my mother lost custody. But I digress. Back to Roland. Did you know dear ol' dad, an avid huntsman, already had a family when the Red Cap curse hit him on a business trip? Married for five years with a four-year-old son. Not that he gave a damn when he chose to cheat on my mother. Did he give a thought to his family? No!" Walden spat.

An all-too-common complaint of those who lost loved ones to the Grimm Effect. "Roland didn't do it on purpose. The curse—"

"Was a convenient excuse," Walden barked. "He

wanted out of that marriage. I might have been young, but I remember my parents fighting. Even heard the word divorce mentioned a few times. But rather than try to work things out, he betrayed us. He fucked another woman and freely admitted it upon his return, which destroyed my mother."

My throat tightened. "I'm sorry, but I swear Mom never knew he was married."

"Would it have mattered?" he snapped. "The curse got what it wanted."

It sure had. Misery to go around. "I guess your parents worked things out since he never came back."

"On the contrary, he planned to return to his whore. It didn't matter how much my mother begged. As far as he was concerned, the marriage was over and too bad for me and my mother. She didn't take the news very well. To this day, I remember the screaming. His, I should clarify. Mom was in the kitchen when he gave her the news. Right next to the butcher block. She took a knife to him. Slit his throat, ear to ear, and she watched as he bled out."

My mom made a noise of distress. Jeezus, how horrifying.

"Roland's dead?" My flat response.

"Very much so. I might have been young, but I still remember the shock on his face."

My stomach heaved. "You witnessed your father's murder."

"It was more like art. The way the blood fountained. How he had his mouth opened to scream, only he couldn't make a sound. He jiggled for a bit on the floor until the loss of blood killed him."

That trauma explained so much. "What happened to your mom?"

"They declared her insane and locked her away. Given I had no other family, they put me with my grandfather, who was too old to care what I did in my spare time. Lucky for me he never listened to the whining neighbors."

"Why did they complain?" I asked in a faint voice.

"They accused me of having done something to their pets. I had, but they could never prove it. Grandad was a hunter you see. He taught me how to properly track my prey and hide my tracks. Took me along with him on his hunts when I was old enough to hold a rifle steady. Unfortunately, even killing monsters stales after a while, so I migrated to more challenging prey."

"You started killing people." I felt faint.

"It was the logical next step. At first, it was about the thrill of the kill. I only went after random strangers. I'd lure them into an alley and slit their throat with a knife. But when I devised my new plan and moved here, I decided to fool those seeking a man with a blade. You saw my early experiments in that hut in the woods."

I'd not noticed the box just inside the living room entrance. Walden bent to reach within, and when his hand emerged, it wore a glove that looked like it belonged with a costume. Covered in long hair and tipped in claws.

"Is that supposed to be a wolf's paw?"

Walden grinned. "Indeed, it is. It's much easier to indulge in my hobby when authorities waste their time looking for something specific. Like, say, a wolf."

Absolutely insane but it did clarify one thing. "You framed Aidan."

"I did. He provided me the perfect patsy. Thanks to all my years spent hunting monsters, I knew he was a wolf the moment I crossed paths with him."

"You've met?"

"Oh yes. When I learned he was a handyman, I hired him to do some work on my office renovation. How ironic he happened to live in the same building as my target."

I made a leap. "You moved here because of me."

His lips curved. "I did. Funny thing is I didn't even have a glimmer of your existence until a year ago. Roland never knew he left his whore pregnant. When my grandfather died last year, I found a box with all the paperwork from my mom's trial. In the transcripts, she spoke of a wicked woman named Charlene who stole her husband. I'll admit it wasn't easy tracking your mother down. Lots of Charlenes in this city, but my perseverance paid off."

"You were going to kill my mother." A flat reply. I kept him talking for a few reasons. One, I wanted to know why. Why target me and those people? Two, I kept hoping for a miracle, which wouldn't happen because I'd dumbly listened to him and come without warning anyone.

"I had such torturous plans for her, but then imagine my shock when I realized she'd had a daughter."

"But you didn't come after me. You went after innocent people."

"Because when I learned you were an agent, I knew it would be fun to draw this out. I targeted people wearing red to taunt you."

"And did a poor job of it. We didn't even know about the bodies you'd stacked in that hut until you reported it."

He shrugged. "A miscalculation that I corrected by making the next targets more public. In the end, it worked. You believed a wolf was killing and targeting possible Red Caps."

"You're sick."

"What can I say? The curse must have been passed down. Now I am the huntsman in this story."

I pursed my lips. "Surely you're aware the huntsman saves Red Cap. He doesn't kill her and her family."

"Which is the problem with the original tale. What did the huntsman gain from coming to her rescue? Nothing. It's a stupid story that needs to change."

"Agreed, but killing isn't the way to do it. I would

know. I've beaten the curse already. All it needs is for you to walk away." I didn't hold my breath hoping to sway him, but I also had to try.

"Walk away?" He sounded incredulous. "Never. You are the reminder of why I lost my parents and had to live with that cold bastard of a grandfather. You are the living embodiment of where my life went to hell. Once you and the whore who tempted my father die, only then will I have peace."

There was no reasoning with this level of insanity exacerbated by the Grimm Effect.

"I'm surprised you're wasting time instead of leaving town. Haven't you heard? The bureau is aware Aidan didn't murder those people. As a matter of fact, given they know it's a frame job, and you were the one who supplied much of the supposed evidence, I imagine it won't be long before they're looking for you." Could I scare him off?

"Let them. I plan to be gone within the hour. Now that you're all gathered, it's time to end this story properly."

He dropped the string he'd been holding this entire time, taking the booby-trapped gun out of the equation. He shoved his now free hand into his box, and it emerged wearing a second wolf's paw. His grin proved quite vulpine and his eyes quite mad as he huskily murmured, "Who wants to die first?"

Before I could even think of replying, Grams lurched from the couch in his direction, unable to walk because of her bound ankles, but capable of throwing herself at him. I gasped as Walden swiped, Grandma only barely lifting her arms in time to block. A claw slashed through the tape binding Grandma's wrists. Not enough to free her but the tear was enough that, when she hit the floor on her knees, she could tear them apart.

"Guess we have a volunteer." Walden lifted his arm, ready to come down on my grams, who threw herself sideways and kicked with her bound feet, causing Walden to teeter.

I saw my chance and dove for him, slamming into his mid-section, forcing the air out of him with an oomph. Our momentum slammed against the kitchen chair with its gun. As it fell, so did Walden, me on top of him.

He snarled in my face. "You're just delaying the inevitable."

"Don't be so sure of that," I muttered as I rolled away from him. The gun had been knocked sideways on the chair but remained attached enough I couldn't grab and use it.

A quick glance showed Grandma had a knitting needle in hand and was stabbing the tape on her ankles. Smart lady. I'd not seen the basket for her hobby by the couch. I dove for it and grabbed another pronged metal stick, not the greatest weapon, but when I whirled with it extended, Walden paused.

We faced off, me wielding a weapon of knitting destruction, him with his mitten claws.

"You can't win, Riding Hood," he warned.

Rather than reply to him, I muttered, "Grams, free Mom and get out of here while I deal with this asshole."

Walden arched a brow. "Is that any way to treat your brother?"

"I like being an only child." I darted for him, slashing my needle, which he easily dodged.

"I always wanted a sibling," he admitted. "The fun I could have had torturing a small child." He sighed and smiled. Sick fucker.

"I can see why your dad wanted to leave," I taunted. "You probably reminded him of his crazy wife."

"Don't you talk badly about my mom," he screeched, launching himself in my direction. I sidestepped and stuck out my feet, catching him in the ankle, causing him to stumble but not fall.

A brief peek showed Grandma had slashed through the tape on Mom's legs first and hauled her to her feet.

Mom's panicked gaze met mine, and I yelled, "Get out of here. Call for help."

"Yes, run, run. You won't get far," taunted Walden. "Your cell phones are in the toilet. And your car... Let's just say it's going to need to be towed."

"Son of a bitch." I darted for him, swinging my useless metal stick, which he danced away from.

"You're a feisty thing compared to the others. In the beginning, I had to drug them because they just wouldn't stand still as I practiced. But as I got better, I managed to kill them before they even knew it was coming."

"Not true. You drugged the father of that family a few days ago. Guess you're not good enough to face a real foe head-on." I taunted him, hoping to distract him.

"Hunters use whatever tools are at their disposal to ensure mission success."

"Those people didn't deserve to die." I inched to my left, closer to the dining room with the buffet, which had dishes I could throw but also the good silverware, which included knives.

"What's the point of being a hunter if you don't have prey? Besides, they served a purpose. Once I mastered the gloves, I needed the bureau to look the wrong way while instilling a sense of panic in you. Did you huddle under your blankets at night wondering if I'd come for you next?"

"No," I retorted. "I dreamed of how I'd catch you and put a bullet between your eyes."

"You feared enough to send your family away."

"Them, I worried about, but me?" I cocked my head and smiled. "You messed with the wrong Fairytale agent."

Slam. I heard a door shutting and, seconds after, the rumble of my bike. Relief filled me. No matter what, Grams and Mom would be safe. They had to be. Now, time to save myself.

I feinted to my right, and Walden fell for it. I spun before he realized my intent and leaped for the buffet. Cutlery jangled as I yanked open the drawer. I had no time to really look, just grab. My hand closed around… a fork.

Walden moved quicker than expected, and I hissed as claws swiped across my arm, leaving stinging stripes. I whirled and stabbed him with the tines.

"Bitch!" he yelled as he reeled from me, the fork sticking out of his arm.

I grabbed a knife next. "Let's go." I beckoned. "Or are you going to slither out of here on your yellow belly because you're not the only one who can cut now?"

"You call that a knife?" he mocked in a poor imitation of Crocodile Dundee. He tossed his wolf gloves to the floor and moved from me to his box and removed an axe. Short-handled, the kind often brought along with camping supplies to chop small branches and split kindling.

Walden held it upright like a torch. "Say hello to the axe that killed the wolf threatening your mother. My father kept it in the trunk of his car, and my grandfather saved it for me. Do you know it's never tasted blood since that wolf? Until today." He swung it pendulum-like in front of him as he sang, "Why what big eyes you have, Agent Hood."

"All the better to see the truth," I replied, taking a step back. His axe versus my steak knife gave me cause for concern.

"My what a sassy mouth you have, little sister," he mocked, shuffling closer.

"All the better to call you an idiot for choosing evil over good."

"My how tiny you are compared to me, whore's spawn," he spat next.

"All the better to outrun your psycho ass," I huffed as I spun and bolted for the front door.

Mom and Grams should be long gone if they'd not fallen off my bike. Hopefully they'd reached the neighbors and called for help. I just had to stay alive long enough for someone to arrive. Meaning, I couldn't let Walden catch me.

It might have been a tad easier if the Grimm Effect weren't involved, because I stepped out of the cozy cottage into a dark and dank forest.

17
Aidan

THE HOURS OF GRUELING QUESTIONS LEFT Aidan exhausted—also mad and frustrated. How could anyone believe he killed those people?

Yes, he could turn into a wolf, something that hit him years ago but that he'd always kept under control. When the wildness in him got to the boiling point, he let off steam by changing into fur and running in the woods, where the only thing he hunted was rabbits.

He'd never attacked a person. Actually, despite his intimidating size, he didn't get into fights. Most people gave him a wide berth. So to be accused of something so heinous...

The pounding at his door not that long after Red left had woken him. He'd fallen asleep, the scent of her lulling him. Still in a state of bemusement, he'd stumbled to the door and opened it to people yelling he was under arrest.

It took the silver cuffs going on his wrists for him to manage a dazed, "What am I being charged with?"

"Murder."

Worse, though, than the false accusation? The look on Red's face as they'd hauled him away.

Did she actually believe him capable? Probably. They'd not known each other long and yet, at the same time, long enough for him to know that he was incredibly attracted to her, not just because of her looks. She was the whole package. Witty. Strong. Stubborn. Sensual. Funny. And she loved gaming as much as him. He'd been having so much fun with her. More than he could have ever imagined.

But that was all over now. Now he sat in a cell, a prisoner accused of atrocities, and he had no idea how to prove his innocence. How could he when whoever framed him had been so deviously thorough? Claiming his truck had been seen in the area of the crime. Stealing his keys, which included those of two clients he'd been doing work for—clients now dead. Leaving bloody clothes in the basement, clothes he'd never seen before. And then the most damning thing, placing his business card with one of the bodies.

"It's bullshit," he'd exclaimed upon being placed in a cubicle for questioning.

"We know you did it," the pompous ass across from him kept stating. Agent Jasper apparently didn't believe in innocent until proven guilty and did everything he could to get Aidan to admit to the crimes.

In vain.

"No, I didn't. I'm innocent. Someone is framing me."

"Sure, they are," Agent Jasper drawled. "Meanwhile we found a dead body with your business card. Just a coincidence, or are you going to claim you went for a walk in the woods and dropped it?"

"Anyone could have," he'd growled. "And I told you, it couldn't have been me. I was with a woman."

"Yeah, we know. She's dead."

"Fuck off already. Blanche is not dead. She fucking works here. Ask her. She'll tell you we spent the evening together. From like nine until midnight."

"I am not bugging Agent Hood with your lies. No way she'd be dating a wolf, not with her history." Said with a sneer.

Except she didn't know about that side of him. He'd not dared mention it. Nobody knew because he'd not wanted to be pigeon-holed.

Agent Jasper kept repeating the same questions just to receive the same answers. Goaded Aiden to no result. Eventually, the agent gave up, claiming, "Maybe some time in our special cage will get you to talk." They dumped Aidan in a silver-lined cell without a phone call. Then again, who would he contact? Red obviously either thought him guilty or wanted to disassociate so as to not ruin her career.

So much for the claim the truth would set him free.

Click. Clack. The sound of heels approached, but he couldn't be bothered to look and see who came to lead the next round of questions. He lay on the bench in his cell, an arm draped over his eyes.

The person stopped by his cell, and a soft feminine voice murmured, "Mr. Malcolm? I'm sorry to disturb you. I'm Agent Jones."

"I already told the last agent everything I know, which is nothing. I didn't kill anyone," he muttered.

"So it appears. That's why I'm here. You're being released."

"What?" He almost fell on the floor in shock. He recovered and stared at the petite blonde standing on the other side of the silver-coated bars.

"While I can't state for certain you're innocent of all the pending charges, it appears that the most recent murder was conducted by someone other than you. A good thing someone reliable came forward to provide you with an alibi."

"Red finally fessed up? Took her long enough," he grumbled.

"I assume you mean Blanche? Yes, she was under the misassumption the killing occurred before your rendezvous. Once she realized her error, she told us it couldn't have possibly been you in those woods and insisted we release you."

"Glad you believed her. I told Agent Jasper hours ago about Red. He accused me of lying."

Her lips pursed. "You told Tyrone you were with Blanche?"

"Multiple times."

"I do apologize. While it's not an acceptable excuse, everyone has been on edge with these murders, and there was much excitement when we thought we'd caught the perpetrator."

"Is this a bad time to mention while I have an alibi for last night, I don't for all the incidents?" He'd probably regret his honesty.

"Did you kill those people?"

"No."

The woman stared him in the eyes and nodded. "I believe you."

"But what of the evidence?" He couldn't have said why he argued.

"Much of it is very convenient, meted out piece by piece, almost as if someone were building a case against you. Do you have any enemies, Mr. Malcolm?"

"Not that I know of." He tended to keep to himself.

"Perhaps a dissatisfied client?"

"One but I doubt he'd go this far."

"You'd be surprised. So am I to take it you do have someone displeased with your services?"

"Yeah. Some dude called me in to do some work on this office space he's renovating. I did as asked, but he complained about literally everything. The paycheck wasn't worth the hassle, so I quit."

His claim had her nose scrunching. "I don't suppose his name was Alistair Walden?"

"Yeah. How did you know?"

"Because Mr. Walden happens to be the source of some of the supposed eyewitness accounts."

"Son of a bitch. Why the fuck would he frame me? It's not like we fought or anything." On the contrary, things had always been very civil, if cold.

"I don't know why Mr. Walden acted in such a fashion, but rest assured, I will find out." She pressed her hand against the electronic pad outside his cell and then keyed in a password. The door clicked, and she pushed it open. "You're free to go, Mr. Malcolm."

"What about this Walden fellow?"

"We'll handle him. Don't you worry."

But he did worry because he couldn't help but recall Agent Jasper's almost constant accusation that he was targeting Red. "Is Walden trying to hurt Blanche?"

"We don't know what the killer wants with her."

"Meaning yes." He clenched his fists as his inner wolf stirred.

Agent Jones cocked her head. "You care for her?"

"It might sound crazy since I barely know her, but yeah. She's a formidable woman."

"I'm glad you recognize that. Blanche might act tough, but she's got a heart of gold."

"Is she still here? I'd like to thank her for getting me sprung."

"She should still be around somewhere. Let me see if I can track her down."

Agent Jones, who told him to call her Cinder, left him at reception while she went hunting for Red.

She returned with another woman, the pair of them looking worried. "Blanche isn't here, and her bike is gone."

"Maybe she went home to get some sleep," Aidan suggested.

The brunette shook her head. "No way. Blanche would never have left without saying something to us." She held out her hand. "I'm Belle by the way. Co-worker and friend."

A very pregnant woman entered through the main doors to the bureau, waving a phone. "Look what I found outside. Isn't this Hood's? She must have dropped it."

"Let me see it, Luanne." Cinder snagged it from the pregnant woman and frowned as she tapped on it. "The screen is cracked pretty bad, but... looks like I can still log in. Good thing I know her password." Cinder kept sliding her finger on the screen, and he noticed the moment her face turned white. "According to her phone log, Walden called her, but she didn't answer."

His fists clenched. "Why would Walden be calling?"

"He's done it a few times, usually to throw you under the bus," Belle stated.

"That's not all," Cinder stated. "Her mom called

seconds after, and Blanche answered. Didn't speak long though."

"Phone Mrs. Hood. See if she knows where Blanche is," Belle suggested.

The call went right to voicemail. Cinder bit her lip. "Might not be anything."

"Bullshit," he exclaimed. "You said it yourself, she wouldn't have left without saying anything unless—"

Cinder's phone rang, and she frowned. "Unknown number," she replied, and her entire face went white after she answered. She murmured, "Stay where you are, Mrs. Hood. We're coming." She hung up and blurted out, "Blanche is in trouble. That was her mom calling from a neighbor's place. She says a man called Walden came to her place and took them hostage. Blanche helped them to escape, but she's stuck there with him." Cinder paused before adding, "He admitted to being the killer."

"Send out an emergency message," Belle barked. "Everyone needs to get their ass to the Hood cottage. Let's move." Belle's quick stride had Cinder hurrying to keep up, and Aidan tagged along.

"Where does Red's mom live?" he asked.

"Just outside the city. But you can't come." Belle tossed the last bit over her shoulder.

"Like fuck. Red's in danger."

"And you're a civilian," Belle retorted. "We'll handle this. You should go home. Talk to Luanne at reception. She'll call you a cab."

"But Red—"

"Will be fine. She's tough," Belle stated before sliding into the passenger seat of a tiny car that wouldn't have fit him anyhow. "Cinder, you coming?"

The tiny blonde bit her lip but nodded before getting into the driver's seat. They put-putted away, and he paced, the wolf within agitated, wanting to follow. However, he had no wheels, no wallet, nothing.

"You look pretty upset for a guy set free," Hannah stated as she joined him in the parking lot.

"Red's in trouble. An asshole ex-client of mine took her family hostage."

Hannah froze halfway into a truck. "Hold on. Say that again?"

"I don't know all the details. But apparently, some guy called Walden is the killer, and he took Red's mom and grandma hostage. Red helped them escape, but now she's alone dealing with that psycho. Belle and Cinder are heading there now."

Before she could reply, someone shouted her name. "Hannah." A big dude emerged from the bureau and strode at a rapid clip in their direction.

"What's up, boss?" Hannah chirped.

"We need to move fast. Agent Hood is in trouble."

"I just heard." Hannah inclined her head at Aidan.

The big dude caught up to them. He glanced at Aidan and muttered, "Sorry if we were rough earlier. Given what we knew at the time, we expected you to fight."

"No worries. Y'all were just doing your jobs." In truth, they'd been gentler than expected, given they thought him a sadistic murderer.

"Can't believe the real killer fooled us so badly. Well, he won't get away with it. Cinder texted us the address where Walden was last seen," the boss man declared.

"It's Red's mom's house. Cinder and Belle are already headed there," Aidan informed.

The big man cursed. "Those idiots. We've got to get there ASAP," he declared, swinging into a blacked-out SUV.

Hannah eyed Aidan. "Sit tight and try not to worry. We've got this. We'll send word once we locate Blanche."

"I don't want to sit around. Can I go with you? I swear I can be useful." He tapped his nose. "Especially if I let the wolf out."

"It might be ugly," Hannah warned as he clambered into the back seat.

It sure would be if Aidan found out Walden harmed a single hair on Red's head.

18

Leaving my mom's cottage, I walked into a totally unexpected environment. It was as if the Black Forest in Germany had teleported my mom's cottage to nestle amongst its gloomy trunks and boughs.

When I'd arrived at her place, the skies showed not a cloud in the sky and the sun shone. Now, however, I found myself in twilight, barely able to see more than a few feet, the shadows almost thick enough to gather.

It might work to my advantage if it could conceal me from Walden. I raced from the cottage, with the psycho following and not even trying to hide. He whistled and sang as he tracked me.

"Where, oh where, has my Red Riding Hood gone? Oh where, oh where could she be?"

He sounded close. Too close. Some might have argued the impossibility. I'd emerged before him, sprinted in a random direction. Still ran. But the

Grimm Effect was out in full force. It wanted me to die, most likely retaliation for having evaded it.

Fuck the curse. I wasn't about to concede, a fervent vow that didn't go unnoticed. As I sprinted, I suddenly found myself wearing my red cape and holding my gram's knitting basket. I halted abruptly and glanced into the woven container to see it packed with muffins and a loaf of bread instead of something useful.

Jeezus.

"Come out, come out, wherever you are," Walden chirped, again closer than expected.

I ran again, only to suddenly emerge to the left of my mom's cottage, somehow having managed to go around in a circle, that or the curse really wanted to force a confrontation.

It wanted us to face off? Then so be it.

I planted my feet and held tight to the basket. A slight breeze ruffled the fabric of my cape. From the forest, Walden emerged, wearing a maniacal grin, axe in hand.

"What do you say we put this story to bed?" Spoken with a spin of the axe, and me with a fucking wicker basket.

As he came for me, I used it, swinging it to smash into the swinging blade. The tip of the axe dug into the crispy fibers, and as he pulled back, it tore apart my only weapon.

The goodies fell to the ground, and Walden

laughed. "Guess grandma isn't getting her treats."

He came at me again, and I feinted, dodged, ducked, but it would be only a matter of time before he connected.

As my cape fluttered, it gave me an idea, and I whipped it from my shoulders. "Here, psycho, psycho!" I crooned as I dangled it like a picador. Like the bull when it saw red, Walden came in a rush, and I swirled the fabric, wrapping it around his arm and axe, giving me leverage to pull.

Walden leaned back, intent on regaining control of his weapon, and missed the boot I aimed at his junk. And I didn't hold back when I kicked.

"Argh." He grunted and recoiled, releasing his grip on the axe.

Holy shit, it actually worked. I scrambled to try and untangle it while he groaned in pain. Only to pause when I heard a click.

I looked up and saw Walden holding my gun.

My fucking gun. I didn't know how or when he'd grabbed it. I'd not seen it when bolting from the house, but he now aimed it right at my face.

"Not exactly how I wanted to end things, but dead is dead. Goodbye, Red Riding Hood."

I didn't beg. Didn't cry. Didn't even breathe.

Didn't want to give Walden any warning as the massive wolf stealthily crept from behind. It had to be Aidan. I'd recognize those eyes anywhere.

I smiled as the wolf coiled its hindquarters to pounce and said, "Have fun in hell, *brother.*"

Before Walden could figure out where I got my renewed confidence, the wolf slammed into him from behind, knocking the gun from his hand. However, my lover, while looking ferocious, appeared to be only pinning Walden to the ground, not ripping out his throat.

Just more proof Aidan was never a killer.

But I was.

I snagged my gun from the ground, and when Walden heaved Aidan from his back and would have fled into the woods, I shot him.

In the leg.

He tried to crawl anyhow, so I shot the other one.

As he lay on the ground, cursing me out, "Fucking whore. I'll kill you. Kill your mother. Your grandmother. Your neighbor. Your—"

I shot him in the head.

Twice.

You should always double-tap pure evil.

And before some said I could have bound him and brought him to the office for arrest... Walden was a dead man the moment he started killing. A trial would have cost taxpayers money. Not to mention leaving him alive, with the curse so heavily invested in him, might have resulted in his escape.

So I handled it. Cold? Yes, but necessary.

Grr.

The wolf growled, and I turned to see him standing, expression wary.

"I'm not going to shoot you, Aidan."

The wolf cocked his head.

"Yes, I know it's you, and for what it's worth, I'm sorry I thought for one second you were guilty of those crimes. The question is, can you handle the fact that I'm the violent one in this relationship?"

The R word emerged, relationship, kind of bold seeing as how we'd only fucked once and met, like, less than a week ago. Still, there was something about this man that made me want to try.

Aidan shifted from massive wolf to man, fully dressed, I might add, because, unlike in the movies, the Grimm magic that caused the transformation didn't ruin clothes.

"Does this mean we're a couple?" he queried.

"Guess you're rethinking our compatibility after this." I waved a hand at the body lying at my feet.

His lips quirked. "Not really. I've seen how you play *COD*. No mercy. No hesitation. It's one of the things I like about you."

"Oh? And what else do you like?" I purred.

"How you're fearless and focused and sexy as fuck."

"You're not bad yourself. Although I do wonder how you found me." I waved to the forest around us. "The curse seemed pretty determined to isolate me with the huntsman."

"Call it instinct. When Hannah parked outside the woods, everyone else was yapping about getting a drone and calling in dogs. But all I could think of was you alone and in danger. So I shifted and followed my nose and instinct."

"I'm glad you found me." I closed the distance between us and reached up to cup his cheek.

"I guess now the question is, how do we find our way out?"

"We don't. While we wait for the curse to get bored and find someone else to play with, why don't we go inside?"

And by inside, I meant my old bedroom. Might as well pass the time pleasurably, as it might be a while before we were found.

We spent hours in my bed. Fucking for part of it. The sensual glide of body on body, the huffing pants, the clenching orgasmic pleasure a welcome to the stress and fear of before.

We also talked. Me revealing my history with the Red Cap curse and how Walden tied into it. He told me how the wolf thing hit him suddenly on a camping trip.

By morning, we'd explored every inch of the other's body and revealed all our intimate secrets. While I knew people worried about me, I wished we could have remained lost a while longer.

Alas, a pounding on the cottage door just after dawn indicated our interlude was finished.

Levi and his Knights, along with Belle and Cinder, came barging in demanding answers. Boy, did we have a whole lot to say.

Aidan had to go to the bureau to give a statement. I had to fill out too many reports, including one that told how I'd eliminated Walden. Then I had to deal with my hysterical mother and my proud Grams, who hugged me and whispered, "That's my tough girl. I knew you could handle him." Unlike my mother, who wailed, "I can't believe you sent us away. Do you know how scary it is to have your grandmother drive?" I would have said exhilarating. After all, she'd taught me how to ride a motorcycle.

My boss gave me a pat on the back and said good job. Levi offered me a spot with the Knights. Belle fist-bumped me and said, "Way to go!" Whereas Cinder sighed and said, "Wish I could meet a wolf who loved me as much as yours does."

Love?

Was that why I grinned widely when I arrived at the apartment building to find Aidan waiting for me outside?

As he swung me around in his arms and kissed me soundly, I'd have sworn I heard a book slam shut.

Epilogue

"Ha. I win!" I crowed, bouncing up from the couch, game remote in hand.

"Only because you kept waiting for me to spawn so you could shoot me again," Aidan grumbled from beside me on the couch, where we'd been playing *Call of Duty* for the past two hours.

"Not my fault you put yourself in a bad spot." I grinned, and he returned it.

Things had evolved in the wake of the Huntsman Murders—the name given to the documentary that spawned within weeks. Aidan's name got cleared when the truth came out, and as an added bonus, his handyman side business had more work than it could handle. I'd gotten a key to the city from a mayor, who was thankful I'd put an end to the killings, and even better, I wasn't currently on my boss's shit list despite having bent some regulations.

While the woods around my mom's place disappeared, Regent Park's forest remained intact and became a hot spot for thrill-seekers. A search of Walden's house turned up all kinds of trophies from his kills, including some from murders in other states. His dog, Rambo, though, appeared to have disappeared. Since nothing dog-related was found in the house—no food, bed or toys—everyone assumed Walden borrowed the pup for his charade.

Mom and Grams remained living in the cottage, but in a surprise twist, both women had decided to stop dwelling on their past loves and get out there again. In other words, Grams was dragging Mom out to bars and clubs, trying to find her a man now that Mom knew Roland wouldn't be returning.

But you're probably wondering about me and Aidan. Things were going well. While we were a couple, we hadn't yet moved in together, but that was only a formality seeing as how we spent every night in one or the other's bed. His mostly, since his king-sized mattress had more room.

"Shit, look at the time. We gotta get ready." I tapped my watch.

"Do we have to?" he groaned. "You know I'm not good with people."

"Yes, you have to, and no whining like a pussy about it. Today, you meet my mom and Grams." I'd waited a month. A month of my mom curious about the man in my life—and time for her to adjust to me loving a wolf. A month of exploring this exciting relationship, which had yet to wane. On the contrary, seeing Aidan made me smile. We laughed. We played. We fucked. We talked. Being with Aidan made me quite simply happy.

Only one test remained.

Meeting my family. I'd held off on it, worried I'd jinx it. Not to mention, I just knew Mom would go overboard once she realized I'd found *the one*. However, I couldn't keep Aidan hidden forever.

An hour later we stood outside the cottage door, which opened to my beaming mother. "Baby girl! So glad you could make it with your beau. I knew you couldn't resist my homemade egg rolls and stir-fried chicken rice."

My stomach gave a happy lurch, and I leaned close to Aidan to whisper, "I swear if you leave me for my mom's cooking, I'll skin you alive."

He snorted. "I'm sure it's not that good."

It was. But I trusted him to not leave me over food. "Mom, I'd like you meet Aidan. Aidan, this is my mom, Charlene."

Mom eyed him up and down before saying, "My what big hands you have."

"All the better to fix things with, ma'am."

Mom tittered. "I love a man who's handy. Won't you come in."

We entered, and it was Grams next who eyeballed my man. "My what big shoulders he has."

I rolled my eyes and hip-checked him before he could reply. "Are we done with the Red Cap puns?"

Grams and Mom eyed each other before giggling, "No!"

And so the evening went.

Aidan's big appetite. All the better to do justice to Mom's cooking.

His big laugh, which even I couldn't resist. All the better to keep the mood light.

But it was on our way home in his truck, with his hand on my thigh when he murmured, "I see where you get your big heart from," that I blurted out, "All the better to love you with."

Yup. I said it.

First.

And what did he reply?

"I love you too, Red, forever and always."

Finally, while it wasn't noticed at first, it turned out Red Riding Hood falling for the Big Bad Wolf put a permanent end to that particular curse. Although, that still left the Grimm Effect with plenty of other stories to pervert.

I'd keep fighting to save those cursed. After all, I knew it was possible to find a happily ever after.

AGATHA CROSSED her arms and glared at the pile of glowing books. It had been decades since she'd found the stone that changed the world. Decades of not aging and trying to reverse what she'd done.

To no avail. The Grimm Effect kept spreading, and now it was mutating. Her fault, of sorts. She'd thought to confuse or dilute the stone's curse by giving it other books. Nicer fairytales, so to speak.

It worked and didn't. The Grimm Effect gobbled up the new words, some of them alternate versions of the original. But did that lessen the effect?

Nope.

The magic grew stronger.

The stories more varied.

Those that remained, that was. Recently, the words to The Little Red Cap tale had reappeared alongside a few other tales in the book. Those that did get inked back had their cursed effect disappear from the world. A glimmer of hope when it came to breaking the Grimm Effect.

Alas, the stories that had been broken hadn't helped Agatha yet. However, she kept hoping because being a fairy godmother to all the budding Cinderellas and Sleeping Beauties of the world was exhausting.

And speaking of... As the magic sucked her into a vortex, which would spit her out somewhere random, she could only hope someone, somewhere, would put a stop to at least one of those stories.

Poof.

As she appeared suddenly in someone's kitchen, a

petite blonde woman stopped feeding a troupe of mice chunks of cheese to say, "Oh no, not you, again."

"It has been a while."

"Not long enough," she muttered.

It took Agatha a bit to recognize the woman since she'd last seen her as a young girl. "Most people would be happy to have a fairy godmother whose task is to make your wishes come true."

The blonde frowned and shook her head. "I already got my wish. I graduated from the Fairytale Academy with honors and have a great job with the bureau."

"But you're still single," Agatha pointed out.

"I'm aware, but that doesn't mean I want or need a prince."

Agatha smiled. "In that case, I've come to the right place."

Are you ready for the next Fairytale Bureau story? *Cinder's Trial* features Agent Jones, followed by *Belle's Quest*.

Made in United States
North Haven, CT
24 June 2024